DEATH BY PASTRAMI

LEONARD S. BERNSTEIN

UNO PRESS

Printed in the United States of America

Leonard S. Bernstein

Death by Pastrami

ISBN: 978-1-60801-027-1

Copyright © 2014 by UNO Press

UNO PRESS

All rights reserved.

University of New Orleans Press

unopress.org

Other Books by Leonard S. Bernstein:

Getting Published
The Official Guide to Wine Snobbery
Never Make a Reservation in Your Own Name
"How's Business?" – "Don't Ask."
The Black Snowman

For Laura, Audrey and Larry

Contents

The Guided Tour of 7th Avenue   11

The Unusual Courtship of Gendelman's Daughter   20

Navy Blue Forever   26

At Home I Would Have Been a Princess   34

Tell Me Where All Past Years Are   43

The Debt   53

Rhoda and the Six Wildcats   67

The Man Who Wanted to Buy a Heart   79

A Gentleman From Sole to Crown   84

Kessler and the Grand Scheme   92

The Twenty-Nine Pens of Simon Englehart   97

The Million Dollar Proposition   106

Krinsky and the Ragman   118

Three Square Inches of Nothing   127

Nobody Beats Mason   137

Death by Pastrami   145

Y-S-L   151

THE GUIDED TOUR
OF 7TH AVENUE

I have agreed to take you to the garment center, and we begin at 7th Avenue and 38th Street where the cutters are milling around at lunchtime. I approach one of the cutters who has been here a few hundred years and say, "How's business, Benny?"

"Terrible," he answers. "Never in my entire life have I seen it as bad as this."

That means business is O.K.

You ask me how terrible can mean O.K. and I consider sending you to Berlitz for a course in a foreign language.

Clack-clacking down the street come the dress racks and the dollies pushed by the blacks and Hispanics. And you ask, "How come only blacks and Hispanics—thirty years ago there were only blacks and Hispanics!—where are the whites?" And I answer that thirty years is not much time in the garment center.

And then you notice that the street signs read FASHION AVENUE, and you ask, "Why is it still called 7th Avenue when that is no longer its name?" And I answer that yes, the name was changed but change does not take hold easily here.

You don't believe me. You ask, why is there no change? You mention Park Avenue and Madison Avenue—the breathtaking skyscrapers, the dazzling shop windows. "And here, pushcarts?" you ask.

I consider how to explain. It is difficult to explain 7th Avenue to an outsider. How to explain civilization standing still?

What the hell, I try. "You want to know why there is no change? Because it takes imaginative people to effect change, and all of them have left for Asia. Do you know how long it takes to get twelve cartons of fabric up to the fifteenth floor of a garment center loft? In that amount of time a manufacturer in China can sew enough dresses to clothe a medium-sized city."

You are astounded. You've heard of Ralph Lauren and Armani. You thought they were here. Where are they? Yes, they are here, as the Taj Mahal is in India, but India is not the Taj Mahal.

You are incredulous. I don't know what to do with you. I decide to show you one of our modern industrial achievements, and we enter 257 West 36th Street where Meyer Kaufman runs forty machines making children's underwear.

I tell you that Meyer runs a pretty smart operation and you tell me that everybody smart is in China. I tell you it's good that you are listening, but there remain two reasons why anyone could be left: because they make highly intricate hand-sewn operations and must hire the old-time workers who still remember how to stitch a buttonhole or turn a collar, or because they themselves are too old to move to Hong Kong. Meyer is sixty-three. Where is he going? he tells us.

How does Meyer compete, you want to know. I am pleased that you are asking intelligent questions, or at least questions that I am able to answer.

"On price and value Meyer cannot compete against the wages in Asia. But there remains customer service. There are a lot of retail stores in New York like Macy's and Bloomingdale's, and sometimes these stores can't wait for a shipment of underwear from Cambodia. Meyer can get fifty dozen over to them on a handtruck within a few hours."

I tell Meyer I am showing my friend the garment center and he smiles, "So what are you doing *here*? This is ancient history."

Meyer is a small man with a narrow, pointed face and thin wisps of brown-grey hair wandering over his forehead. He is nervous, and makes quick, mouselike movements, as though he fences jewelry and the cops are closing in. He welcomes us but says he only has a half hour. The union agent is coming up at 3:30—they have a labor dispute to settle. Meyer laughs. "A million garment workers in Taiwan and China. No unions and no labor disputes."

We walk out into the shop. There are two long rows of sewing machines with operators facing each other, mostly Hispanic in bright flowered dresses, their hands and fingers fluttering over the garments. "Piece work," Meyer says for the benefit of our guest. "They get paid for how much they produce."

Alongside the rows of sewing machines is a long wooden cutting table with about nine inches of fabric piled up. The cutter says hello and we shake hands. The index finger is missing— not uncommon. Left-handed cutter, I think. The cutters don't lose fingers from the hand that guides the machine. It's the other hand, the one that holds the fabric in place in front of the spinning blade. The hand that guides the machine grips a wooden handle behind the machine, always out of danger. The other hand is brought around in front of the blade and presses down the nine inches of fabric. The blade spins forward into the V-shaped opening formed by the thumb and index finger.

In an accident it is usually the index finger. There's an old joke that if you went to visit Local 12, the cutter's local, and didn't know where you were, you could find out quickly by shaking hands.

There's a scissors on the table and I grip it to just confirm my notion. It's a left-handed scissors and I think back twenty years to when I first arrived in the garment center and didn't believe there were left-handed scissors.

Meyer says to the cutter, "Kroloff is coming up at 3:30. I'll send Mary in to let you know when he arrives. Then I'll walk out here with him, both of us together."

The cutter returns to work and Meyer starts to explain—stops—starts again. Is clearly pained. "We have to set things up when Kroloff arrives. Sam can't see ten feet in front of him. Take a look at his glasses. Madame Curie didn't have lenses like that when she discovered radium. Sam can see up close; he can see the pencil marks that guide the cutting knife, but he can't see far. If Kroloff finds out, Sam is retired on the spot. So we have a warning system. We identify Kroloff before he gets close enough to notice the problem. That way Sam gives him a big hello and Kroloff doesn't realize that Sam can't see who he is saying hello to. Today I'll walk in with Kroloff. Sam will vaguely make out two figures and right away he'll shout hello Kroloff. When we get closer he'll know because Kroloff is six inches taller than me and Sam can make that out, so he'll reach out to shake hands with the right person."

"But the cutting blade…surely. And he's lost one finger already."

Meyer sighs, as though why am I bothering him with something he already knows. "Sam lost his finger thirty years ago when he could see perfectly. Thank God it didn't happen here. You know, they don't lose fingers because they can't see. They lose them because they think they're hotshots and don't need to drop the guard in front of the blade."

We're back in Meyer's office. The phone rings. We turn to leave. Meyer raises his hand to say wait. Kroloff is delayed. "Sit down," Meyer says, "we can talk a while."

Meyer is tired. His eyes are bloodshot from the dust of threads and cotton shavings. He slumps in his high-backed chair, behind him a window, framed with the thin silver tape of an alarm system.

"Just as well. It's about Sam. I can't pay him the standard cutter's hourly wage any longer. Kroloff says I have to. The union contract…something like that. What do I care? The thing is, Sam is good but of course he can't see. I have to give him a helper for anything over ten feet. The helper always has to be around. And of course he gets paid. If you add the helper to Sam, their combined wages make Sam the best-paid cutter in New York."

"Why can't you explain this to Kroloff?"

"Because if Kroloff suspects anything about Sam's eyesight he'll stop him from working. Maybe he's right—how do I know? The union has too much at stake. If it would ever be discovered that the union had a cutter on the job with 200/200 vision it would make the newspapers. And can you imagine what they would say about the finger? Kroloff would get indicted. I would get indicted. There would be a whole investigation. You know how those things are. The newspapers get it, it will sound like the garment center uses only blind cutters."

"What does Sam say?" I ask.

"Sam says pay him less and don't let Kroloff near him. What else is Sam going to say? This is the only company on the face of the earth where he could work."

"It's you and Sam against Kroloff," I mutter, thinking that the issue defies any labor problem I've ever heard of. "What about letting Sam go and hiring a competent cutter? Sam's old … he can't see …"

Meyer nods, conceding the sense of that. "Sam's old; he can't see. I'm old; I can't see so good either. A new cutter? What will I say to him after all these years?"

At that moment a young lady, slightly agitated, rushes into Meyer's office. "Kroloff is in the shop, talking to Sam," she says.

"How did he get in?" asks Meyer, but he doesn't wait for an answer.

We sit there quietly, not knowing whether to stay or to leave. In five minutes Meyer is back in the office. "Kroloff is walking around the shop, talking to the operators. He'll stop in my office in a little while and I'll introduce you."

"Shouldn't we leave now?" I ask.

"You wanted to show your friend the garment center; this is the garment center. Wouldn't you like to meet a business agent?"

Within fifteen minutes Kroloff walks into the office, a large bear of a man, enormous hands—meat-packing hands. Could have been a wrestler, maybe.

Nice smile though—hellos all around.

"So how do things look, Kroloff? You think I'm ready for a computer?"

"Not bad, Meyer; you run a good shop."

"So maybe one year I'll make a profit?"

"A few things, Meyer," and Kroloff turns toward us.

"Friends," Meyer says. "Say whatever you want."

"Josie claims that you have her sewing bottom ruffles and she can't make out. She says you took her off hemstitched sleeves and put her on ruffles, and she wants to know when she can go back on sleeves."

"She can go back when the stores want hemstitched sleeves. Right now they want ruffles. Am I responsible for the style changes in America?"

"What can I tell her, Meyer?"

"Tell her as soon as we have hemstitched sleeves again she will be the first one to get them. I don't know what else to tell her."

Kroloff jots something down.

"You remember, Kroloff, in the old days we argued over the minimum wage. We argued over piece work prices and Saturday work and time-and-a-half for overtime. We argued over *something*. Now we argue over hemstitched sleeves which went out of style five years ago. You remember you used to holler about the price of groceries and how could workers survive on what we were paying? We argued that the Southern factories were paying half as much as we were, and how would we compete with that.

"Two o'clock in the morning—we fought till two o'clock in the morning! Name calling. Everything. No time-outs. You once marched out of this office and said the shop was on strike. We said go ahead, we're closing down the business anyway."

"That was a long time ago," Kroloff says.

"Now we fight over whether Josie works on bottom ruffles. In China nobody works on bottom ruffles—they do it with an automatic machine. The automatic machine doesn't know the difference between bottom ruffles and hemstitched sleeves. In China they have machines that cut automatically. A laser beam follows the pencil marks. Here we fight over whether Sam should have an assistant."

Kroloff smiles and nods. He stands, and I think, "The Man with the Hoe." *Bowed by the weight of centuries...*

"What about Sam?" he asks. "You think maybe he'll retire?"

"I think maybe I'll retire," says Meyer.

Kroloff says good-bye, turns toward the door, "You know, Meyer," he says, "we are taking a terrible chance."

* * *

It is four o'clock in the afternoon and we are standing at 7th Avenue and 36th Street. The operators are emptying out of the buildings, chattering and laughing, speaking rapidly with their hands. The cutters follow, moving more slowly—a caravan of grey cardigan sweaters—each one complaining that nowhere in the world is there a job as bad as his.

I ask if you know what that means, and you answer that means his job is O.K.

We look for Ralph Lauren; he's not here. He must be uptown having cocktails at The Four Seasons. We look for Calvin Klein. He must be in Paris, designing a new line of jeans. We look for fashion models, but this is 7th Avenue and 36th Street; there are no fashion models here.

I turn to see if you are disappointed and think maybe I should have done this differently.

"This is the garment center," I tell you, not knowing what else to say.

We walk another block or two. The sun is setting over 7th Avenue and the buildings grow cold and dark and morbid, the same way they have for as long as anyone can remember.

THE UNUSUAL COURTSHIP OF GENDELMAN'S DAUGHTER

It was no surprise in the community that Gendelman's daughter had never married. She was painfully unattractive. Nor did she pay any attention whatever to her appearance or dress, acting out of some strange spite, as though God had made her ugly and she would show Him how little she cared.

Like the town beggar or the town fool, she was known to everyone. Women whispered behind her back, and children bandied her name in their jump-rope rhymes.

Years and years of hurt had made her tongue bitter and her attitude defensive. She twisted around every kind word, so that people finally felt it wise to leave her alone.

Gendelman loved her deeply and sensed her pain. One of the wealthy merchants of the village, he would have given her any amount of money to buy clothing or jewelry. He knew that she had a kind heart and a keen mind. Indeed, when Gendelman traveled to buy merchandise, his daughter ran the business as well as he did.

Gendelman never despaired and always had his eye open for eligible young men. A part of him still believed that somewhere there was a man for his daughter. Considering the evidence, only a father's love could so color his vision.

Marriage brokers in other cities were sought out. Young men were wined and dined. And it was understood that an immediate partnership in Gendelman's business came with the hand of his daughter. But everyone who came to see her said that the situation was hopeless.

"You will marry her, Gendelman, only to a cripple," they said.

Little did they realize the truth of the statement, for Gendelman was a realistic man, and had started years ago to look for young men who were not in possession of all of their faculties.

And it happened one day, in a town not more than twenty miles from Gendelman's home, that a young man was pointed out to him whose foot was so terribly twisted that his whole body convulsed when he walked.

The man was a beggar, but Gendelman had been informed that his parents had been substantial people and had died when the boy was an infant.

That night Gendelman had dinner with the young man and was impressed with his candor and with his certain sense of dignity. But the situation demanded the most delicate handling. Over a warm dinner and a glass of wine, Gendelman convinced the young man that he had known his father, and convinced him further that he would be wise to come to Gendelman's store where he would be given a job as a clerk. Not that it required much convincing. The beggar had not had a warm meal in two weeks.

Gendelman explained that it would be inappropriate

to bring the young man back with him, but asked that the young man arrive at his store the following week and ask for a position. Gendelman gave the beggar money to buy clothes and transportation, and bid him good night.

So that the following week the beggar was seen hobbling along the streets of Gendelman's town, moving in the direction of his store. So crippled was his walk that the children on the street stopped their games and turned to watch him.

"You're just right for Gendelman's daughter!" one of them shouted, and the others laughed in agreement.

Gendelman hired him as they had arranged, and put him to work tallying the inventory and checking the invoices. To his other employees and to his daughter he explained that the unfortunate young man had in fact been a beggar, but that Gendelman had known his father and felt a sense of obligation.

The young man learned the business rapidly and in a number of months was given increased responsibilities. This brought him in contact with Gendelman's daughter to whom he was particularly kind out of appreciation to Gendelman. And Gendelman's daughter, having found someone as ill-blessed as she, was very responsive.

In fact a strange thing was happening. On occasion, Gendelman's daughter came to work with her hair combed. And once even wore a dress with pretty yellow flowers.

Even more strange, the young man had visited a doctor and was doing exercises for his foot—and his walk had improved noticeably.

All of this did not miss the sharp eyes of Gendelman, who walked around the store whistling and smiling, and of course saying nothing.

But so naive were these two that they watched each other from afar and could never summon the courage to speak about anything more intimate than inventory counts. Both considered themselves so hopelessly inadequate that they could not conceive of being attractive to the other. Years and years of living with their ugliness had buried any normal response deep inside each of them.

So Gendelman decided that something had to be done.

A man wise in business may not be so wise in understanding a daughter who has been ugly all her life, nor a beggar with a club foot. Gendelman might have let time run its course. Or he might have dealt with intermediaries. But he didn't.

One day he called the young man into his office and spoke to him about his daughter. The young man was embarrassed but grateful for Gendelman's advice. He admitted that he loved the daughter, but confessed that he could see no way that the daughter could be interested in him, nor did he ever dream that he could aspire to the hand of the owner's only child.

Gendelman dismissed his reserve and urged him to act, pointing out that he, Gendelman, was getting older, and the store would one day belong to whoever married his daughter.

Ah, Gendelman, seasoned in the old ways. For years he had searched for the young man who would consider his daughter, and now he had found one who loved her. It exceeded all hope. How trivial it seemed to Gendelman to offer him a partnership, when for his daughter's happiness no sacrifice would have been too great.

The offer seemed quite all right to the young man, although in truth he was more interested in the daughter than owning the business. And so, after spending a day rehearsing his lines, the young man abruptly asked the daughter for her hand in marriage.

This caught Gendelman's daughter so completely unprepared that she could not understand it at all. Marry her? It was inconceivable.

And then, slowly, it seemed to come into focus, and she asked the young man if he had been in to see her father.

She raced home, her mind visualizing the worst. Her father had sought out and brought back for his daughter a clubfoot. She was not good for anything else.

She tore into the room where her father was sitting and hurled the truth at him.

"He has told me everything," she said.

Gendelman was caught by surprise. He tried to comfort her but the situation was beyond him.

His daughter was crying desperately and she ran upstairs to her room.

It took the young man a few more minutes to drag himself to Gendelman's house. He pounded at the door of the daughter's room but she shrieked and would not let him in.

"It is sometimes best," said Gendelman, "to let her cry. Perhaps she will get over it."

But he was wrong.

She didn't get over it, and when they knocked on her door early in the morning they found her sitting in a chair in a strange state of melancholy. The village doctor was summoned at once but could find nothing wrong with her. And doctors brought in from the surrounding towns and cities confirmed his diagnosis.

She remained in her room for a number of days and then slowly began to move about. At which time those who were close to her noticed that she could only walk with the most terrible kind of limp.

NAVY BLUE FOREVER

Henderson was in trouble thirty seconds after he knotted his first four-inch tie. The tie looked terrific but his shirt collar was too narrow. So he went out and bought three new shirts. The shirts complemented the tie, but there was now something wrong with his suit: the lapels were too narrow. So Henderson went out and bought a new suit.

The suit was snappy, but the belt loops were much wider than his old suits and his belts wobbled around. So Henderson threw out the old belts and bought some new wider styles. It didn't take him long to realize that the wider belts no longer fit through the loops on his older suits.

Five hundred dollars poorer, confused and frustrated, Henderson prepared to hang himself from the chandelier with his fashionable four-inch tie, and just then an idea struck him.

"Why do I have to be more fashionable?" he thought. "What does fashionable do for me? Does fashionable keep me warm? Is fashionable more comfortable? Does it pinch less or breathe easier? Are there more pockets or does it dry clean better?

"What fashionable does," thought Henderson, "is keep me poor."

The idea gripped Henderson with such intensity that he made a vow. He vowed that he would find a single outfit, and that he would wear nothing else—no other combination—for the rest of his life.

He looked in his closet and found a basic navy blue suit. It seemed to be the suit to fit all occasions, and so he decided that it would fit all occasions, and went to look at his shirts. He had striped shirts with narrow collars and solid shirts with button-down collars. He had pink shirts and white-on-white shirts, and a lavender shirt that the salesman had told him was the new color. He had worn it once.

Some of his shirts had French cuffs and some had button cuffs. Some of the button-cuff shirts had two and three buttons, just in case—maybe—one button couldn't keep it buttoned.

Henderson noticed that he had one plain white shirt with a button cuff and he decided that he would wear that style shirt for the rest of his life.

That meant he would no longer need cuff links. Henderson examined his cuff links. He had large onyx cuff links to match his new four-inch tie and wide lapels. He had small porcelain cuff links, hand-painted by the monks in a monastery in northern Italy. He had a pair of Florentine gold cuff links with his initials engraved on them, just in case he forgot his name. And he had one pair of plain silver cuff links that were about the size of a dime. Henderson threw all the cuff links into a brown paper bag and put them on a high shelf.

So he had chosen his suit and his shirt, and that would make it easy to choose a tie. He opened a closet where his ties hung from little silver spokes, about fifty of them. He had club ties with alligators and rep ties in twenty colors. He had ties with designer's initials at the bottom. He also had solids, checks and dots—big dots and little dots. And he had one hand-painted tie with a horse's head.

Henderson chose a solid red tie—closer to a wine color—and stuffed the other forty-nine ties into the brown paper bag.

Then he looked at his tie clips. Henderson had a lot of devices to hold his ties in place. He had stick-pins and chains, and he had the standard tie bars with designs on the bar. One of the designs was an engineer's compass. He had asked the salesman to show him something fashionable, and the salesman had asked what he did.

"I'm an engineer," said Henderson. So the salesman reached behind the counter for the engineer's tie bar and handed it to Henderson. He bought it, but it had always bothered him. He failed to understand why his profession needed to be announced on his tie clip.

Finally, he tossed the collection in the brown paper bag, holding on to one tie bar, straight across and nothing on it.

Socks were simple. He had socks to match each of his suits, also some plaids. He smiled. From now on he would need only black to match his navy suit.

And of course, he would need only black shoes.

He was so elated with the decision that he called Greta and told her all about it. Greta listened quietly, realizing that discussion and debate were not called for, but she told Henderson that she would be right over.

"Some of these ties that you're discarding are quite stylish," she said. "Look at this one. With a blue shirt and your grey plaid suit this would be quite fashionable."

"Why do I want to be fashionable?" asked Henderson.

Greta paused. Nobody had ever asked that question before. It was obvious why everyone wanted to be fashionable. To be fashionable.

"Well, you'll look better," she said. "And people will be more impressed with you. And you'll have more self-confidence."

"People will be more impressed if I'm fashionable?" asked Henderson.

"Certainly," said Greta.

So Henderson stuffed Greta in the brown paper bag and put her on the high shelf. Well no, he didn't actually, but he was thinking about it.

From then on, Henderson only purchased articles of clothing that fit his new standard. He didn't throw out his old shirts and suits, but as they wore out he replaced them with the new standard. So that over the next six months, his wardrobe narrowed to the point of being almost one outfit.

It took about six months for anyone in the company to notice. Henderson worked for SKM International, a huge public corporation mainly in the computer field. He worked with seven other engineers, none of whom might be described as fashionably dressed, but all of whom varied their attire a little, usually not more than they felt was absolutely necessary.

In the sixth month, someone mentioned Henderson's getting an awful lot of wear out of his suits, and Henderson decided it was time to tell.

"No variation at all?" someone responded.

"None at all," said Henderson. "If I want a shirt I call the Macy's shirt department, tell them the style number and size, and they send one right out. Better yet, I do the same thing with my shoes; I call Florsheim, give them the information, and then just pick them up. I don't even have to see them.

"I used to go to the shoe store and spend an hour trying on different styles. Now I have no problem. All I need is a telephone."

The other engineers nodded their heads recognizing the logic and good sense of Henderson's position. But they remained unconvinced.

"The idea is good," one of them said, "but there ought to be a little variation. Otherwise it gets boring."

"Who's bored?" said Henderson.

"Well, I think you might be. Supposing you applied the same reasoning to food. Every day of your life you would have lamb chops with string beans and potatoes. That wouldn't be much fun."

"You're right," answered Henderson, "but that's because I like food and I enjoy the variety. If someone else didn't enjoy variety then he might be quite satisfied with the same dinner every night. And he'd probably save time shopping and save money by buying in quantity. I like food, but I don't like clothes. I can't see any advantage in wearing different combinations."

Henderson's logic was unassailable and his associates were both impressed and thoughtful. Being men of limited sartorial interest, they responded at once to the idea, but somehow couldn't quite digest the whole dose.

"Once in a while, I'd like to wear a different tie," one of them said feebly.

But Henderson had six months of dedication behind him and he responded at once.

"What brand of undershirt do you wear?" he asked.

"I wear Jockey T-shirts, large size."

"Do you wear anything else?"

"No, that's all I wear. They fit me very well. I stuff them all in a drawer, and every morning I pull one out. Why would I want to wear anything else?"

"Well, then...?" said Henderson.

The seven engineers turned away, mumbling. Not one of them was ready to narrow his already narrow wardrobe, but each of them was convinced of the sanctity of Henderson's position.

During the next three months Henderson's wardrobe finally narrowed to the uniform. People called it just that—somewhat unjustly—out of pique and irritation. Many wished it had been their idea or that they were at least courageous enough to do the same thing. And of course, Henderson had become the subject of every coffee break, with those lining up for him and those against him, but nobody yet following him.

Certainly not Mr. Rathbart, the vice-president, who called Henderson into his office one day to find out what all this nonsense and commotion was about.

"Henderson, you are not exactly inspiring confidence among your fellow workers. Your conduct is irregular, disruptive and suspect. I'd like to know when I can expect you to be over this thing."

But Henderson had long since realized that he would be called in by Rathbart, and he was able to explain his position persuasively. He pointed out in particular, that when he had started at SKM, some fifteen years ago, any nonconformity was approached with a fairly rigid attitude.

"You might say that the germ of this idea began right here, in these very offices."

Rathbart scowled, "Regardless of where you learned it, I want it changed."

"Then you are telling me that unless I change my position I will no longer be permitted to work for SKM?"

Rathbart thought about that for a moment. Would he dismiss a man on the grounds that he wore exactly the same outfit to work every day? It was, after all, neither immoral nor incompetent.

"I want it changed, Henderson. It is disruptive to the company. But if you're asking about dismissal—no, it is not grounds for dismissal."

So Henderson left the office. By and large, he had won again.

In time, the coffee breaks found new and more scandalous gossip to occupy the time, and Henderson's navy blue suit and red tie became a common and accepted sight around the office.

People grew tired of the debate, and actually they grew tired of Henderson. Little by little, his friends and business associates drifted away, not out of anger or irritation, but just worn out by the endless discussion and by the whole affair.

The irregularity of Henderson's position had become regular, and the argument, for all its intellectual conviction, had become a grand bore.

Worse—slowly and imperceptibly—Henderson had become the mirror image of their conscience. He became the small voice of morality: the tiny pull of good against the forces of evil.

Every time someone came to work in a smashing new suit or a stylish tie, there was Henderson, wearing the same goddamn outfit he would wear forever. Every time someone fussed and bothered, and maybe felt pretty good about the way he looked, there was Henderson, exposing by his very presence, the pretention and the pomposity.

So Henderson became the symbol of good sense and reason; the pure, unrefined, unblemished, uncontested statement of virtue.

And when the guys got together to down a few beers at the tavern, and when they traded stories of excess and indiscretion, there was Henderson in his navy blue suit—in his habit—in his robes.

It was too much for anybody to bear, and in time Henderson drifted away into his own private world of sanctimony and honor. And he and his navy blue suit lived in that world for the rest of his days, content and convinced, but terribly lonely.

At Home I Would Have
Been a Princess

In the old days of the garment center, like the old days of the automobile, the sewing machines were cranky, lumbering contraptions, always shaking and rattling, and always breaking down. Each one had a personality and we matched the personality to the operator. The sassy young black women worked the ruffle machines. God, they could make those old machines play Dixieland—their hands and fingers fluttering over the garments, and miles of ruffles floating through the needles. The old shrivelled Jewish and Italian operators belonged to an earlier generation. Always bitching, and always unhappy, they worked the hemstitch machines. Slow, tedious, petulant machines, the marriage was perfect: the machines bitched, the operators bitched; the machines rattled, the operators rattled.

And then there were the Puerto Ricans. Not as fast nor as graceful as the blacks, they seemed to have a certain precision. We trained them on the zigzag machines attaching lace to necklines and bodices. I particularly remember the Puerto Ricans, a young, spirited, handsome group of women—and of course I remember Elena.

I hired Elena myself. We had a hand-scrawled sign, HELP WANTED, hanging by a frayed wire near the freight entrance on 28th Street. A fourth-grader could have printed it more neatly. But you didn't print HELP WANTED signs neatly in those days unless you intended to pay a living wage. Maybe uptown they printed neat signs. I don't know; I never worked uptown.

Elena appeared one day—rode the freight elevator up to the ninth floor, no doubt fighting off the elevator operator—and asked for a job. I went to the foreman (also mechanic, also cutter, also shipping clerk in an emergency) and asked what we had for a young Puerto Rican; in a single sentence discriminating on the basis of age and ethnic background. We didn't think about those things then. We had a job, we had a machine, and we were all trying to make a living on the ninth floor of a fairly filthy, incredibly hot loft in downtown Manhattan.

I admit to being aware of Elena the moment I saw her. It was that dark, smouldering, Latin loveliness. Her black hair tumbled all over her shoulders and over the white seersucker dress that hugged her body as though muslin had been pinned and fitted to a size thirty-four form.

She was incredibly proper, her dress not unlike a nurse's uniform, sleeved and buttoned to the neck, and yet clearly containing a shape that didn't belong locked up in all those buttons and pleats. The sensuality was overpowering. I had grown up with fair-skinned, well-groomed Jewish girls, wearing white middie blouses with orange ties on assembly days, their code of honor strutting three feet ahead of them. They could discuss Gide and Thomas Mann, and find meaning in Ezra Pound. And I don't mean to say they weren't attractive. But attractive is one thing and smouldering is another. Elena exuded the very perfume of womanliness.

I will confess that I began to seduce her that moment with the very first words of warmth and concern, and for three years I never stopped.

The first rule in a garment factory is: no fooling around with the operators. There are always young, attractive, and probably available women—it's an industry of women—and from your first day somebody makes it clear that if you want to fool around that's fine, but not with the workers. So if it was seduction, it was seduction from afar. It was suggestion and inference, and nothing was ever going to happen.

I would like to say that it stopped there, a discreet glance, an offhand compliment, even a bit of extra attention, but it didn't stop there. I would design styles that brought me to Elena's machine, where I could stand behind her and look over her shoulder as she sewed the garment, and of course at the opening of her blouse and the slow gentle curve of her body. And I took her loveliness home with me, into the night, into my dreams, into the most cunning of my fantasies. Never a word passed, never a hint, never any banter, but she knew—she had to know—from the scent, from the feel, from the tension in the air around her.

* * *

In the shop she was extremely proud; too proud I thought, almost arrogant. It was, after all, 28th Street in the early 1950s; nothing much to be proud about. But the Puerto Ricans had a special pride, as if to say, "I may be a garment worker here in New York, but at home I would be a princess." And that was written all over Elena, in the way she walked, in the way she dressed, and in the way she worked. Especially, perhaps, in the way she worked. Other operators worked only as hard as they had to, their feeling being that it was them against the company. The company would take as much as it could and they would give as little as they could. The foreman could holler and they would give more, but they kept track, and sooner or later they would slow down and get it back. It was the classic confrontation of the bosses and the working class: two armed camps slugging it out in a war that started at the beginning of time.

It had nothing to do with Elena; she worked out of a sense of dignity. It was *understood* that she gave her best. To have pushed Elena would have been an insult. I must say, that among hundreds of things that I did not understand in those days, I understood that. I understood Elena's sense of pride and she knew I did.

I cannot really tell you how badly I wanted to touch her. She sensed it and knew she had that over me. So if she was my slave in the ancient ritual of the production line, I was her slave in an even more ancient ritual. She understood that also, more than I did, and she would lightly brush against me and smile, as if to acknowledge the delicate balance that existed between us. She could recite it all with a twist of her shoulders, causing the grain of her blouse to tighten against her marvelous breasts, and she knew that I was listening.

Still, she never teased, she never beckoned. As if to say, "I know how hard this is for you and I cannot help that, but I will not make it harder." There was that strange, tenuous, unspoken relationship: Elena in control of my life force and treating it with understanding. I in control of her machine, in control of her livelihood, and yet making it clear that I knew who she was. Not much of an exchange perhaps, unless you knew how much I ached to touch her and how much she ached to be a lady.

To Morris, the foreman, she was just another worker, just another machine, and you could see with what contempt she looked upon him. It wasn't that he was cruel, it was just that a lifetime of working in steaming garment factories had drained the sensitivity from him. And he *also* had a master—he was slave to the day's production schedule, and the machines and operators blended together. Indeed, I think he had more respect for the machines, which at least showed up for work every morning.

The mistake he made was in giving Elena style 749—a tedious and difficult lace application—and then underpaying her. In those days, you see, we paid operators by the dozens produced: the more they produced the more they earned. An operator might be paid 20¢ a dozen for a lace neck operation, so that she would make $20 a day if she produced 100 dozen. The object was to pay as little as possible so the operator would work as hard as possible. After all, if we paid 17¢ a dozen, the operator would have to produce 118 dozen to earn the same $20.

The objective for the operator was to work as slowly as possible so as to make the operation seem more difficult. Then, perhaps, the company would pay 23¢ a dozen and she would have to produce only 87 dozen to earn her $20. Somewhere within this time-honored charade a correct price was arrived at, usually with much complaint and distrust on both sides.

It didn't happen that way with Elena. She always worked as well as she could and she assumed we knew it. So when Morris paid her 17¢ for the lace neck operation instead of the 20¢ she deserved—and when Morris pushed her to work faster—the steam built up inside that lovely body. Still she tried, working that treadle faster and faster, racing to get her bundles from the bins, cursing the broken needles. Still she tried, not for Morris and not for me, but because she would not surrender and have to *ask* for more money. But one day it exploded: Elena complaining bitterly that *nobody* could earn a living at 17¢, and Morris shouting back that if she couldn't he could find lots of unemployed zigzag operators who would welcome the chance.

My god, Morris, how could you have said that? Out of what depths of sullenness and insensitivity could you have said that to the proudest spirit in the shop? Had you no sense of abuse? No sense of violation? Could you not understand that this was not management but insult?

Elena stood up at her machine, defiant, staring at Morris as if to say that if this was at home in San Juan she would have him flogged within an inch of his life. But this was New York, on a line of thirty sewing machines dripping oil, with bathrooms behind a curtain on a string, and with toilets that were as often clogged as not. Where Morris, who also swept the floor and cleaned the machines, was boss, was padrone. She turned to him, out of control, pointed her finger and shouted so that the whole shop could hear, "You son of a bitch!"

The machines froze, the shop became silent, and all eyes turned to Morris. Whatever his crime, nobody called the foreman a son of a bitch. Nobody.

I don't think he knew what to do; I think it was beyond him. But thirty women turned toward him and sixty eyes were saying, "O.K., big shot, what are you going to do now?"

And of course there was only one thing he could do. He told Elena she was fired.

At that moment I arrived at the scene. "She called me a son of a bitch," Morris said, as though that was the end of the matter. I turned to Elena. She didn't say a word but fixed me with a look that said, "I don't have to explain to *you*. You know who I am."

I understood at once, and I was certain she was right, but there was no way around the insult. If Elena stayed, Morris would be the laughingstock of the factory.

I called them both into my office. Morris was stunned but not angry.

He didn't want to lose Elena either; he was paid for production units. And he didn't care about the insult, not for himself, but he understood that he could not go back into the shop. Elena was silent, looked at me with those wide-open eyes, a little sad, a little lonely, but with pride bristling all over her.

"You don't have to leave, Elena, but you have to apologize," I said.

She looked at me incredulously.

"Elena, I don't want to lose you—I don't want you to lose your job—but what you said was wrong."

Not a word. She rose from her chair, went back into the shop, presumably to collect her things.

"Let me talk to her alone, Morris. Get sort of lost."

I asked her back into my office. The heat had subsided a bit and her eyes had become softer. She was incredibly lovely and I was aware that even in this terrible moment of insult and misunderstanding, I was making love to her. And even when I rose from my chair to put a hand on her shoulder—to try to be responsive—it was a seduction, almost a lechery. Nor was I unaware of the rise and fall of her body underneath that starched cotton blouse.

She understood it all and her eyes said to me, in a clearer language than her voice ever could, "You know what happened. Why aren't you on my side? Why aren't you a man? You are a man when you approach me and I honor you by understanding your desire and anguish. So now, against this pitiful little fool of a man, why are you not on my side?"

I just looked at her—beautiful, spirited, sensuous—but she shook her head, no, and she rose to leave. It was four in the afternoon.

"I come to say good-bye before I leave," she said.

At five o'clock everyone had gone. I was sitting at my desk when Elena came in.

"Please," I said, "just an apology. Try to understand. An apology; it doesn't mean anything."

She only looked at me, softly now, and then her fingers moved to the top button of her blouse and she unbuttoned it. And then, without taking her eyes from me, she opened all the buttons and the blouse spread apart. She took it off and laid it neatly over a chair, and stood before me in a simple white bra, very full and with the fullness rising over the narrow lace edges. And then she reached behind her back, shrugged her shoulders, and the bra fell to the floor.

She stood straight and proud, her breasts very full, very firm. And she stood there without moving, without saying a word, for what must have been five minutes, although in my memory it was five hours or five days. She could have been a princess in any country of the world.

There must have been a moment when I leaned forward in my chair or perhaps started to rise, and she very slowly shook her head from side to side.

And then finally, she reached to find her bra, not bending over but doing what seemed like a deep curtsy—and never for a moment taking her eyes off me.

She smiled then, just for a moment, then slid into her bra, reached behind for the clasp, stood still for a moment longer, and then put on her blouse.

My mouth was cotton-dry and I felt like a little boy. I had no idea what to do or what to say.

"Please stay," I tried. "Please stay here on your zigzag machine." And although I didn't say it—"And let me be near you."

But she turned away, walked to the door, and I never saw her again. Except in my dreams.

Tell Me Where All
Past Years Are

The Crown Derby porcelains might have been worth a million dollars. That's what my sister Elise said, but she was a girl, and girls don't know anything. Besides, she was only nine years old, too young to make a considered appraisal of antique vases. I was twelve and sophisticated. I said they were worth ten thousand.

"Each one, or both together?" challenged Elise, knowing full well that I hadn't given the matter any thought.

"Each one, of course," I said.

As we grew older we often talked about the Crown Derby porcelains, always guessing how much they might be worth. And although our estimates descended from the stratosphere, we always guessed a lot of money.

The porcelains were two matching antique vases, milky-white in tone with tiny figurines swirling among the curves and folds. They rested on two cherrywood coffee tables near the center of the living room. When visitors came they remarked at once about the beauty of the porcelains, so that it almost became a game, when people arrived, to see how long it would take until they were noticed.

Mom and Dad fussed and preened over the vases. They were the jewels of the house, of our lives, perhaps. I remember when Aunt Mildred visited from Pennsylvania, and when she didn't notice the vases (or did notice them and didn't respond properly) that Mom and Dad had plenty to say about the style of life in the state of Pennsylvania, and a few things to say about Aunt Mildred in particular.

Mom often talked about the Crown Derby porcelains, telling Elise and me how they had been passed down from our grandmother, and why they were so valuable.

"How valuable are they?" I always asked.

"Extremely," Mom said.

"Would you say that they are five times as valuable as the mirror?"

I knew the mirror had cost five thousand dollars because I had overheard Mom and Dad talking about it. It thus became my private standard for learning the value of things. If I could get Mom and Dad to relate a price to the mirror I would have it immediately.

"They're much more valuable than the mirror," Mom said, tactfully avoiding a head-on comparison.

You could see the glow on Mom's face when she talked about the porcelains. Even when she skirted around my questions you could tell that she enjoyed being asked, and enjoyed even more saying, "*much* more valuable."

I don't think Mom knew exactly how much they *were* worth. We had owned them for fifteen years. They were fine china and china had soared in value. Friends would ask if Mom had had them appraised, but Mom only motioned aside the suggestion, as though checking the specific value of something so elegant was to demean it.

That's what Mom implied, but it's not what Mom was thinking. She was damn interested in the specific value, but just a little bit afraid to hear it. If it was frightfully high it would worry her, and if it was low it would depress her. Better to leave it alone—better to commit it to that twilight zone of euphoria where facts and figures and realities are unwelcome visitors.

I once noticed a news story which said that a unique Limoges vase had brought $17,000 at auction, a record for a piece of this size. I raced home and showed it to Mom, who smiled but didn't comment.

"Is ours worth as much as that one?" I asked, recognizing the futility of the question, but knowing that Mom didn't mind a bit being asked.

Mom just folded the clipping and put it in the dining room drawer near the silver. Next week she would slip it out and show it to Aunt Sarah. You could show things like that to Aunt Sarah; it wouldn't be bragging.

Of course Elise and I were told never to discuss the Crown Derby porcelains with any of our friends, and we never did. Or at least, I never did. I'm not sure about Elise. I'd guess that she never did either because Mom's request made sense. You don't go announcing all over the neighborhood that you have priceless antiques in the living room. Besides, the porcelains belonged to all of us, and Elise and I felt our own sense of pride in them. I will admit though, that the temptation to tell was sometimes overwhelming.

I remember when fat Monroe Myerson moved into the corner house at Bedford and N. He hadn't joined our punchball game fifteen minutes when he announced that his house had cost forty thousand dollars. We all knew how much houses cost; in those days that was a fortune.

I was about to grab Monroe by the ear and drag him into our living room and show him the Crown Derby vases.

"See that, you dummy," I would say. "They come from an emperor's palace—they're priceless—you can't buy them for any amount of money."

That's what I wanted to say but I didn't say it. It was an unfair restraint to exercise on a twelve-year-old punchball champion.

Fat Monroe and I grew up together in the Brooklyn of the 1940s. Actually, he wasn't a bad kid, but he could be an awful pain in the ass. Every time his father brought home a new 98 Olds, Monroe would prance around and act really stupid.

I didn't care about the Olds because I had something better and I knew I had something better. No product of a Detroit assembly line could stand up to antique china. The only trouble was that you couldn't park the antique china in the driveway.

Elise and I once discussed who would get the Crown Derby porcelains when Mom and Dad passed away. I said that I should get them because I was older. Elise said she should get them because she was a girl and girls understood things like antiques while boys didn't know the first thing about them. I lost the argument and ran outside to play punchball, but that discussion about girls-get-this and boys-get-that has cost her plenty over the years.

And the years did roll by quickly. Mom and Dad sold the house on Bedford Avenue and moved to an apartment on 27th Street. Naturally the Crown Derby pieces occupied the center stage in their living room, and they remained there until last year when Mom and Dad bought a condominium in Miami. The weather and the pace and the danger of New York had finally gotten to them, and they felt they could live more comfortably and peacefully in Florida.

Elise and I helped them move, which might appear an easy job since they were in their seventies and lived in a simple three-room apartment. What could be there to move? Well it seems that there was fifty years of junk: photographs, mementos of a trip to Saratoga, dishes, papers. The first night Elise and I didn't move a thing. We just stood there and looked at everything. Every time I bent down to touch something Mom said, "No, don't touch that, it's a souvenir from Atlantic City," or "don't move that, it's a painting your Uncle Arthur made for our 30th anniversary."

Elise and I left, promising to come back and help them move when they decided what they were moving. For a month they didn't decide.

And then one day, Elise received a call from Mom, who said that she had called an antique dealer and was going to sell off all their valuable old stuff. Mom had heard from Aunt Sarah that the dealer was very reliable and that people had sometimes received surprising offers on things they thought had little value.

I was upset by the whole idea. Why do they want to sell off the mementos of their lives, I wondered. What are they going to get, after all, for Uncle Arthur's painting?

I asked around and friends just told me that old people are very strange and unpredictable about things like that.

It was no secret that both Mom and Dad were particularly tight. Neither of them had ever taken a taxi, and both of them had photographic memories of every bus line in the city. O.K., that was their business; old people are strange and unpredictable.

Another strange thing happened; I got a call from Elise.

"I called Mom today," she said, "and wanted to stop over there tonight but she wouldn't let me. I can't tell you why but there was something odd about it, something she was holding back."

"Well, what do you think it might be?"

"I have an idea; it's pretty far out, but I'll tell you. You know Aunt Sarah recommended that antique dealer. Ever since then Mom has acted very curious about it. I keep asking what she intends to sell and when the dealer is coming, and she's always evasive. There's something that she's hiding; something she's embarrassed about."

"You don't think she would sell the porcelains, do you?"

"No, I don't think so," Elise said. "I think they're just embarrassed about trying to get money for all the old junk that they've accumulated over the years. I think they have in mind to try and sell Uncle Arthur's painting and the Atlantic City cup and saucer set, and they're just ashamed to let us know that they would do that for a few bucks."

"For godsakes," I said, "a dealer won't offer them fifty cents for the cup and saucer."

"I know," Elise said, "That's the problem. That's what they're embarrassed about."

We hung up, but I was terribly uneasy. I called Elise right back. "Let's get into Brooklyn right away," I said.

"Look, if they want to sell their stuff they have the right to sell it. It's theirs. It's not ours. If they wanted us there they would have asked us."

"I'm going to Brooklyn," I said. "If you want to come I'll pick you up in ten minutes." But Elise didn't want to come.

I was in Brooklyn in an hour, and Elise had been right about the whole thing. Mom and Dad were having coffee with this guy in a plaid flannel shirt, sleeves rolled up: the antique dealer. It wasn't difficult to guess; there were open cartons lying all over the place.

Mom and Dad were smiling. The antique dealer was smiling. Nobody seemed particularly glad to see me, but nobody seemed upset either.

"Mr. Hassourian, I want you to meet my son, Leonard." And I shook hands with a little squirrel of a man, quick in his movements, gold-rimmed glasses, dark skin, Lebanese maybe.

"Mr. Hassourian was recommended by Aunt Sarah, and we have had a very nice discussion. He has given Dad and me some good prices for things that we really don't want to drag along to Florida. He has already taken most of the pieces down to his truck and now we are having some coffee."

It took my eyes only three-fifths of a second to land on the spot where the Crown Derby porcelains used to be.

"The porcelains, Mom. What about the porcelains?"

"Oh, Mr. Hassourian gave us a very nice price for the porcelains."

Too late. An hour earlier and I could have stopped them. Forty years they've lived with the Crown Derby porcelains and they sell them to the first dealer who walks in. Did they even check the price? Did they even get an estimate? Did they even—I guess I was asking myself—talk to Elise and me about it?

My mouth got dry and I didn't know what to do. It would have been terribly wrong to ask the price, nor could I try to cancel the sale. I did manage to say, "You're sure, Mom, that you wanted to sell the porcelains?"

"Oh yes," she said. "We have no use for them and they *are* worth money. It's not cheap to live in a condominium in Florida."

I really couldn't tell what the hell she was talking about. I couldn't understand selling a lifelong treasure, something they had been proud of owning for forty years.

"If your mother doesn't want to sell the vases she can certainly keep them," Mr. Hassourian said.

Now I was really confused. Hassourian offering to let them renege on the vases. That doesn't sound like he stole them. What was happening here?

I didn't know what to do, so I did nothing. But I did realize that I would have to get the price from Hassourian. He had one more trip to make and I said I would help him. I said good night to Mom and Dad and we loaded the elevator.

Hassourian had a truck downstairs with lots of blankets and cushions on the floor. "Your parents are lovely people," he said.

"Listen, Hassourian," I said, "You don't have to tell me this, but how much did my parents sell the Crown Derby porcelains for?"

"The two matching vases? Three hundred dollars. But they're not Crown Derby porcelains."

"The hell they're not," I said. "They're Crown Derby porcelains. We've owned them for forty years."

"That doesn't make them Crown Derby," he said. "But I'll tell you what. If you want them for the price I paid I'll give them to you. I actually overpaid your parents for them. When I come to an old person's home there are always one or two pieces that I must overpay for in order to get the other things. The porcelains seemed like pieces that were very dear to your parents. I offered a high price right away so I would not offend them and so they would trust me on their other pieces. This is the way it is with old people.

"There is another thing you should understand," he continued. "Your parents didn't sell me the porcelain vases for three hundred dollars if they were worth six hundred. Your parents aren't fools. They live in a nice apartment and have always lived very well. They know the value of things. If the porcelains were Crown Derby they would have brought them to Sotheby's. They would have gotten an appraisal. Nobody sells Crown Derby porcelains to a small dealer like me."

I stood there and listened. Hassourian was right, of course. I thought back to Bedford Avenue—the porcelains commanding center stage like Lunt-Fontanne. It was a lot of years to think back to and my eyes filled with tears.

"But why…?" I stammered. And Hassourian understood.

"Ah why," he said. "Because we all live fragile lives. We all have our Crown Derby porcelains. Your parents inherited the pieces and at once a mystique grew up around them. Someone said they looked like Crown Derby and they became Crown Derby. Why not? Do we not become what we would like to be?

"And then," Hassourian said, "it was too late to change. Reality, like beauty, is in the eye of the beholder. Could your parents admit now—now that they are in their last years—that the Crown Derby porcelains were a fiction? Indeed, you should understand that it is this very reason that your parents didn't give you the vases, nor did they want you here when the vases were sold. This was the only way for them to end the story of the Crown Derby porcelains."

I took out my wallet, but Hassourian said, "They are yours if you want them but I don't think you want them."

I thought about it and nodded—Hassourian said good-bye—and the Crown Derby porcelains rolled away on the truck. A piece of my life rolled away with them, but Hassourian was right: it was the only way for the story to end.

THE DEBT

The family of Raskin and the family of Melnick lived under a curious arrangement. Every year, when the wheat crop was harvested, Melnick piled one hundred bushels on his wagon and carted them over to Raskin. It never changed. Generation after generation stacked the same wooden baskets of wheat and traveled a road that had been traveled for seventy-five years. The faces changed in the two families; the horses changed that pulled the wagon; but the hundred bushels of wheat never changed nor did the old worn dirt path between the houses of Raskin and Melnick.

Town records showed that on rare occasions drought or pestilence had wiped out the wheat crop. In such years the debt still remained, and the old wagon could be seen bumping around the countryside, buying a dozen bushels from a neighboring town and then traveling on until the wagon was loaded. And it was during such a year that Melnick began to question why the debt had to be paid.

In those times and in that part of the world, the question was sacrilege. Most of the daily life of the village was determined by custom. Friends were friends because their fathers were friends. Enemies were enemies because their houses had always been enemies. The poor bowed to the rich and remained poor. The baker's daughter married the blacksmith's son and the ceremony of courtship was stamped with the approval of generations.

Never mind if the baker's daughter fell in love with the merchant's son. Never mind if the merchant's son returned her affection. Their eyes met from afar and their hands never touched, and one day the blacksmith's son would notice the baker's daughter, and all heads would nod in approval. Things were to be, in the town of Vilna, exactly the way they had always been.

So it was strange and maybe frightening that the idea had crept into Melnick's head that the debt had gone on long enough. But once entered it would not leave, and one night he discussed it with Sarah.

"We have carried wheat to Raskin for three generations," he said, "when does it end? Why are we responsible for an arrangement made seventy-five years ago?"

"It is a debt," Sarah answered, "it has always been a debt. Nothing has happened to change it."

"But I didn't incur the debt. Suppose I decide it is no longer a debt. Who is to say I am wrong?"

"It would be a shame on our house if we didn't pay it," said Sarah. "Everyone in town knows it is our obligation."

Melnick bit his lip and glared at Sarah, and Sarah knew that nothing would ever again be the same. His mind had crossed a bridge and he would never come back to the other side.

"I will find a way," he said. "One way or another I will find a way," and he stormed out of the room.

During the next few months Melnick thought of nothing else but the debt. It weighed upon his back like a thousand stones. It grew out of proportion and he began to see it as a form of slavery from which he would do anything to escape. But he could not simply stop paying it. Sarah was right; the debt was recognized in town. Raskin would bring the matter to the council of elders and Melnick would be ordered to settle his accounts.

And so, out of frustration, Melnick decided he must go to the house of Raskin and discuss the debt with him. But it was not a discussion that Melnick really wanted. It was a trade. There had to be something that an old farmer like Raskin wanted more than his hundred bushels of wheat. Melnick would find out. He would make Raskin a deal. He would find a way.

Raskin was a bit of an old fool. He could be talked to. He could be tricked. And after all, Melnick figured, why shouldn't he take advantage of Raskin? Hadn't Raskin's grandfather taken advantage of Melnick's grandfather? How else could the debt have stood for seventy-five years and three generations?

So one evening Melnick rode the wagon over the dirt road to the house of Raskin, and after the appropriate greetings and good wishes, Melnick opened the subject of the debt.

"I come to your house, Raskin, to discuss the debt, which has now been paid by my family for three generations. It is my feeling that this is long enough and that the obligation should be finally satisfied."

"But we both know," said Raskin, "that the debt has no termination. We both know the agreement."

"Nobody knows the agreement any longer. It is buried with our grandfathers. We must look at it today and decide what is fair."

"Perhaps that is true," said Raskin, "but who shall decide? Surely not you and I. I suppose we must bring it to the council."

"I had thought, Raskin, that we could work it out between us. You are known to be a fair and honorable man. I am known to be a fair and honorable man. Neither of us will take advantage and both of us recognize how unfair is a debt that can never be paid off."

"If such a debt was unfair," said Raskin, "then it would not have been agreed to by our grandfathers."

It was a difficult point to debate and Melnick tried a new approach.

"I recognize that you will not simply surrender the hundred bushels of wheat and wipe the matter clean. I recognize that you will want something in return and I only ask that you be generous in your request."

Raskin thought about the proposal and remained quiet for a long time. He was, in fact, a generous man. He was thought of, in the town, to be slow-witted and a little peculiar. He lived alone, minded his own business, and was rarely seen at the celebrations that marked the important days of the year. Children told funny stories about him, and said he had strange powers. But mostly, in the town of Vilna, he was respected as an old man who liked to be alone, which was not regarded as a bad thing to be.

Finally, Raskin turned to Melnick and said, "I will agree to this, so that the debt shall not follow beyond us. I will agree that the number of bushels of wheat will reduce by five bushels every year until there are no more bushels to be paid."

"But that will take twenty years. I will be paying it all my life. It's not fair."

"In ten years the debt will be cut in half," said Raskin, "you will only pay fifty bushels. And in twenty years it will be finished. It will have ended with you and me."

"I can't agree to it," said Melnick, "I was sure you would propose something more equitable."

Raskin was disturbed. He thought he was being generous and he felt his generosity was being ignored, even being ridiculed. His eyes narrowed and his brow furrowed, and he said to Melnick, "Come back tomorrow night at the same hour and I will have a new proposal."

So Melnick left, and did not even once consider that the first proposal was fair. He was certain that Raskin would do better or that he could be led into doing something better, and the following night he returned to Raskin's house.

Raskin seemed remote and mysterious that second night, and as Melnick began the conventional greetings, Raskin immediately raised his hand as if to say "enough."

"You requested a new proposal, Melnick, and I am prepared with a new proposal. Naturally I am not prepared to simply surrender one hundred bushels of wheat properly owed to me each year at harvest time, but I am willing to make a trade. From this day forward we will divide the land of your farm in this manner: All things that are found above the soil line will be yours. All things that are found below the soil line will be mine."

Melnick was startled. The proposal was unusual. But then again it was also clear and easy to define. The wheat would all be his; the hundred bushels would not have to be paid. Anything below the soil will be Raskin's, but there was nothing below the soil. There might be silver or gold or some precious stone, but nobody had ever found such a thing in the soil of Vilna. And even if it were found, and it belonged to Raskin, the wheat crop would all belong to Melnick and the debt would be paid forever.

It was a marvelous deal, Melnick thought, so the papers were drawn and their names affixed at the bottom, and from that moment on, the worms and moles and the groundhogs and the gold—if there was any gold—belonged to Raskin.

Sarah did not share her husband's enthusiasm for the deal. She had a dull feeling of uneasiness. "The land that we stand on is no longer ours," she said.

"Not so," said Melnick, "the land is ours. The soil is ours; I would never give away the soil. What is found in the soil is not ours. The terms are very specific. It's like giving away the sky above the land. What is found in the sky could be his and what would it matter? Nothing is found in the sky. And remember, the debt is paid. After three generations, the debt is paid."

And so it was, because the next year Melnick harvested his wheat crop and no wagon traveled the dirt road to Raskin's farm.

But the year after, a strange thing happened in the town of Vilna. Two weeks before the wheat crop was to be harvested a dark cloud moved toward the town, heralding a storm. The people hurried inside and closed the shutters, some of them watching the cloud through slats and openings. It settled like some ship from outer space on one of the farms and in fifteen minutes the wheat stalks were gone and the farm was bare earth. The cloud moved from farm to farm and broke up into smaller clouds. In a few hours the town of Vilna looked like it had just been plowed in the springtime. The cloud of insects lifted and disappeared but there was not a stalk of wheat standing.

The people of Vilna had never seen or heard of anything like it. Nor did they know what to do. They settled down for a long hard winter, digging into their savings, taking odd jobs in the neighboring towns, making do. And all the time thinking about next year's wheat crop and the possibility that it could happen again. But it is human nature to believe that tragedies do not recur, and in the spring of the following year the land was again sown with wheat. Here and there a farmer would plant a stand of corn or a patch of cabbage or a row of potatoes—just in case—but by and large, in the late months of the summer, the town of Vilna turned straw-colored as the wheat crop grew toward harvest time.

For Melnick and Raskin the tragedy had been equally severe, but in a strange sense Melnick had profited. In former years he would have been obligated to deliver one hundred bushels of wheat in payment of the debt. Whether he grew the wheat or bought it in another town was not Raskin's concern, and if the debt was still owed, Raskin would have had his hundred bushels. But no more. Raskin had "whatever could be found below the soil line" of Melnick's farm. That was nothing, and Melnick congratulated himself that however great the disaster, he had at least made a wise trade, saving himself one hundred bushels of wheat and surrendering nothing.

The summer drifted by and the people grew tense and anxious. And two weeks before harvest time, when the baker's son was picking raspberries just outside of town, he looked into the sky and saw a dark grey mass moving toward Vilna. He raced back to town screaming, "The cloud!" and the people of Vilna knew that they had been cursed again.

When it was over, the wheat was gone and the ground was earth-brown. Nothing resisted the invaders except a few rows of potatoes, and only potatoes because they grew where the insects couldn't get to them—underground.

And so it was decided by the farmers who stayed in Vilna that next year they would have to plant potatoes if they wished to have any crop at all. And one day soon thereafter, a messenger appeared at the house of Melnick and left him a small note. It read:

WHATEVER IS FOUND UNDER THE SOIL IS MINE.

–*Raskin*

Most of the farmers felt that they could scrape through the winter one more time but for Melnick the disaster was double-edged. Even if he could scrape through the winter, there was nothing he could plant in the spring. Whatever grew above the ground the insects would get and whatever grew below the ground Raskin would get. So he set out to devise another scheme to trick Raskin into changing the debt another time.

He appeared at the house of Raskin one night and he pleaded his case, pointing out how unfair and brutal were those terms which prevented him from harvesting anything on his land.

"But when you accepted the proposal," Raskin said, "you thought that you would be free of your debt and that I would receive nothing in return, did you not? So you agreed to a deal that promised you everything and promised me nothing and you offered no objection. Only now, when the deal reverses itself, do you come to me with your complaints."

There was little Melnick could say except to point out how long their families had known each other and to implore Raskin to find new terms. And Raskin told him to return the following night.

The following night Raskin proposed two arrangements. First, he again offered Melnick that the debt return to one hundred bushels of wheat, reducing itself by five bushels each year. Second, he proposed that the wheat debt be considered paid but that Melnick would bring to the farm of Raskin his next-born son and that his son would labor on Raskin's farm for ten years.

Melnick immediately turned down the first proposal. Why that wasn't any better than Raskin had proposed before. But the second proposal—that was interesting—because Sarah could not bear children and although they had been married for twenty years, and although they had tried for twenty years, no child ever graced their home. So the papers were drawn and the signatures were marked in ink and dried. And Melnick once again owned whatever was found in the soil below, nor did he owe any wheat to the house of Raskin.

But the next year Sarah noticed a change in her monthly cycle and soon her stomach grew round and full, and nine months later, in their twenty-first year of marriage, a child was born in the house of Melnick, and he was named Aaron.

In spite of the debt there was a great celebration in Vilna, as might have been expected when a childless couple bears a boy after twenty years of marriage. There were feasts and songs and dancing in the village square and all of the people of Vilna wished Sarah and her husband good luck and many years of happiness. And Raskin wished him the same good luck but ended his note in this way:

WHEN THE BOY GROWS TO BE FIVE YEARS OLD HE WILL COME TO THE HOUSE OF RASKIN.

Five years is such a long time, thought Melnick. Raskin could be dead in five years. We could move away. Anything. Right now I have my wheat, I have my land, and I have my son.

But five years passed quickly and Aaron grew to be a handsome child and very much the delight of both parents. And when he was five he began to carry the water and do little chores, and one day a message came from Raskin: IT IS TIME.

Melnick knew he would never surrender his only son to Raskin. It only remained how to avoid it. If he had to, he would run, and if he had to, he would fight and maybe kill, but he would never give up his son. But really, Melnick figured, he would find some other trade that would appeal to Raskin, and this time, finally, the trade would work out for Melnick.

And when Aaron grew to be five, Melnick arranged to meet Raskin one night in the same room where they had met twice before.

"I can guess why you are here," Raskin said.

"I've come to make a trade," said Melnick. "Surely you will not take a child away from a happy home. Certainly there is something you will accept instead."

"When you made the trade," said Raskin, "and I returned the produce of your soil, what did you think you were giving me in its place? Did you think, even for a moment, that your farm was being returned, and that you would have to pay nothing in exchange? Or did you think that Raskin is an old fool and has tricked himself out of his wheat and his soil, because surely you did not expect or intend to deliver your son?"

"I was sure you would be reasonable," said Melnick.

"Would you have been reasonable?" asked Raskin. "If you did not bear a son did you intend to resume sending your wheat?"

"I didn't give it much thought, but I do have a fair proposal to make. If you leave me my son I will accept your offer to start paying one hundred bushels of wheat, reducing the debt by five bushels a year. It was your own proposal."

"It was my proposal five years ago, but now I am older and I need someone to help around the farm. Aaron is a strong young boy and I want him in my house."

"You cannot have him," screamed Melnick, annoyed at Raskin's intransigence. "You cannot have my only son. Find something else. Find another trade."

"Then you will not honor the debt?" asked Raskin.

"I will die before I give up my only son," said Melnick.

Raskin sat quietly for a long time, rubbing his beard, scratching his head, and finally told Melnick that he must return the following night. And the following night Raskin outlined his new proposal, which was a very strange proposal indeed.

"There is nothing I would rather have," he began, "than your son, and I am inclined to offer no change in our arrangement. You owed me the wheat, and that was not good enough for you so you urged me to trade for the soil. Suddenly the soil became valuable so you didn't like that trade and you urged me to trade for a child, which you were certain, would never exist. The child exists so that trade is no good and now you insist on something else. You have a curious sense of equity, Melnick; you believe in an arrangement only if it favors your side. When I surrendered the hundred bushels of wheat I did not know that only potatoes would survive on the farms of Vilna. And when I surrendered the soil I did not know that a son would be born to your house. I took a chance and it went my way. You are a greedy man, Melnick, and I must treat you as a greedy man. I offer you, therefore, my final proposal. You may choose between two things but your choice will stand, come what may. I offer you first, in exchange for your son, that we return to the debt of our grandparents and that the house of Melnick owe the house of Raskin one hundred bushels of wheat every year at harvest time."

"Indefinitely?" asked Melnick.

"Indefinitely," said Raskin.

"And my second choice?"

"Your second choice is that you grant me ten years of your life.

"We will agree in writing that your life is to be ten years shorter than it would otherwise have been and that those ten years are bequeathed to me, making my life ten years longer. That is all."

Melnick was stunned. What a bizarre proposal—we trade ten years of our lives. But who are we to trade? Lifetimes are not governed by the living. We are not free to say you shall live longer and I shall live shorter. And if we said it, what would it matter? Raskin is making a deal for something I cannot give and he cannot get.

It crossed Melnick's mind that Raskin had made deals before for things that could never materialize, but it seemed apparent that trading years was no trade at all. Even if he died young it would have nothing to do with the agreement; he would simply die young. And even if Raskin died a very old man, it could only be that he was destined to die a very old man. So Melnick drew his third and final agreement with Raskin and traded ten years of his life instead of one hundred bushels of wheat.

Life went on in the town of Vilna in the traditional patterns and Melnick went about his business. Every day he thought about the arrangement and every day he dismissed it as a silly thing. And then, one day, Melnick became ill. "So what if I am ill," he thought, "everybody becomes ill and everybody becomes better. My illness is not controlled by Raskin."

But he did not become better.

Days drifted into weeks and doctors were brought in from the neighboring towns, but they had no advice and Melnick became worse and worse. Deep lines set in his face and his hair turned white. His skin became pale and day by day he found it increasingly difficult to move his arms and legs. One day, when it became apparent that he might die, he called for Raskin and Raskin came to his home.

"Give me back my ten years," he begged, "and you may take anything that I own."

"It is not in my power to take away or give back ten years of life," said Raskin, "and even if it were in my power I would not do it because I would be taking those ten years from my own life."

Melnick begged and Raskin listened, but no agreement was made and very soon thereafter Melnick passed away. He was buried in the cemetery just outside the town and all the townspeople remarked about the very strange circumstances that surrounded his death.

Of course everyone in the town of Vilna knew that Melnick had traded ten years of his life, but hardly anyone believed that was anything but foolsplay. Melnick died when he was destined to die.

Here and there a few elders recalled how curiously each change in the arrangement had brought about the most unusual events. When Melnick traded the soil below, only the soil below could bear fruit, and when Melnick traded his unborn son, only then, after twenty years, could Sarah bear a child. But they were accidents, of course. Surely Raskin didn't bring forth the insects and surely Raskin could not divine fertility.

So the debt was forgotten and the strange events were forgotten and the story of Raskin and Melnick became one of those folk tales that old men in the village tell to their sons and grandsons. The only curious thing was that Raskin lived in good health into his ninetieth year, a matter of concern and wonder to all the townspeople of Vilna.

RHODA AND
THE SIX WILDCATS

It was a partnership conceived in heaven.

Belkin—expansive, everybody's best friend, excited over all possibilities.

Sharnik—the money man, conservative, intimidating. Calculating business probabilities in the year 2010 with frightening confidence.

Belkin and Sharnik. The chemistry was perfect. So opposite were the partners that there was nothing to argue about. There was no meeting ground. They moved in their orbits as though in different solar systems. It was not even the Moon and Earth, not even a gravitational pull. Not even winds and tides.

Business partnerships, like marriages, often have a curious symmetry. Sometimes opposites work; sometimes they fail. Belkin and Sharnik worked. No one knew why.

They were hardly ever together. Not even when the accountant came to discuss the year-end results. Only Sharnik sat in at that meeting. Belkin couldn't understand the figures. Not even when the Woolworth buyer visited the showroom. It was understood that Sharnik, with his grim attachment to charts and numbers, was to stay away from buyers. Insurance? It was Sharnik's job, of course. Designing? It was Belkin. Sharnik couldn't get his pants to match his jacket.

Yet there was an unspoken feeling. Alone they were incomplete: a jigsaw puzzle with half the pieces missing. Together they functioned. And along with them functioned a small pajama business, tucked away on the fourteenth floor of an industrial building in downtown Manhattan. There they managed about thirty sewing machines, a cutting table and some storage bins, and year after year produced enough flannel pajamas to call it a business.

That was during the late 1930s, a time when the garment business in New York was beginning to unionize. And one day a rather burly—but not threatening—union organizer stopped by the fourteenth floor to talk to the partners. There was not much to talk about. The union was strong. The pajama company was weak. The reality was that the union arrived and the shop signed up. Belkin told the organizer that he would consider the situation and get back to him.

"Let me hear from you next week," the organizer said as he left.

Belkin looked at Sharnik, and Sharnik looked at Belkin. They had never encountered the union before, and it frightened them. The landlord they could deal with. A difficult employee they could handle. The bargaining and the hustling and the yelling and screaming of the garment business was second nature to them. But a union. What was a union? Who was this stranger that walked into their shop and told them what they had to join?

"Listen, Belkin, maybe you ought to handle it. You'll take this guy out to lunch—you'll have a few drinks—and you'll tell him that next year we'll give it some thought. He's right up your alley. You'll ask about his family; you'll tell him business is terrible. You'll buy him a present; maybe you'll slip him a little something."

"I was thinking," Belkin said, "that it's your type of thing Sharnik. This guy wants us to sign a contract with clauses and rate schedules and minimum wages and group classifications. After five minutes I won't understand what he's talking about."

"So I'll understand," said Sharnik. "What good is understanding?"

"You'll negotiate with him. You'll make a deal."

"I don't want a deal. I don't want a union."

"Sharnik, my friend, a union we got. The only question remaining is how much it will hurt."

For three hours they talked about who would handle the union because they were both terribly frightened. It was the first time in ten years that they had ever talked about *who* would handle something. One of them just handled it. But this was new, and it was urgent, and the conversation became cross and then bitter. And after three hours Belkin and Sharnik were not talking to each other at all.

The contract was signed. That was inevitable. Nobody in New York during 1939 said no to the union. And life with a union became an everyday thing in the pajama shop and the partners learned to live with it. But somehow they could not learn to really live with each other. Their fear of the union and their shame of being afraid created a rift that would not close.

There was at that time in their employ a young man named Otto. No one knew exactly what Otto did. Mostly he did odd jobs. He would sweep the rags and the fabric shavings. He would bring cartons of heavy flannel up the freight elevator to the fourteenth floor. He might get lunch for Belkin or run an errand for Sharnik. It was all Otto was capable of; he had the mentality of an eight-year-old.

Everyone liked Otto and everyone felt good about his having a job there. So when Otto put the pajama boxes in the wrong bin or brought the coffee back with cream and sugar when he had been told for the tenth time that it should be black, he was always forgiven. Sharnik, calculating his budget, often felt that Otto was expendable, but he couldn't bring himself to do it. And Belkin, who loved all things that moved and breathed, certainly could not dismiss Otto. In truth, Belkin and Sharnik both felt that keeping him was sort of a good deed, and one that they could afford to do.

It was sometimes difficult to find work for Otto. If given the wrong job it could take days to unravel his errors. One week Otto was put in the sewing room to help move the bundles. The machine operators, all women, would do the seaming on three dozen pajama pants, and then the bundle would move to the worker doing the next operation. The bundles were heavy, and it was wasteful to have an experienced operator move her own bundle when she could be sewing. This week it was Otto's job to move the bundles. It was difficult to go wrong. A bundle moved from Mary to Josephine or from Betty to Rhoda.

The trouble started with Rhoda. Probably the fastest operator in the company she was nevertheless hotheaded and volatile. You could never be sure what was bothering her. She could explode over a trivial thing: the windows should be open or the windows should be closed. They would have asked her to leave years ago but she worked the crucial feed-off-the-arm machine, the most unusual and complicated machine in the shop. It might take months to replace her. On that Wednesday afternoon, as Otto was placing some pajamas in a corrugated carton sitting right up against her left thigh, Rhoda jumped away from her machine and screamed, "Don't you touch me!"

Otto backed away and thirty pairs of eyes focused on Rhoda. "He tried to grab me!" she screamed. "He molested me. I'm quitting right now unless you fire that idiot!"

Well, this was a serious matter. It was bad enough to lose Rhoda, but what about Otto? They couldn't have someone around who would frighten the women. So Belkin immediately sat down with Rhoda trying to calm the situation.

"Listen, Rhoda, he's just a boy—you know what he is. I don't even know why we keep him; he makes so many mistakes. I'm sure he bumped into you—he's so clumsy. Maybe he even..."

But Rhoda had already hurled her challenge. How could she back down? "He tried to grab me. He's some kind of sex maniac."

"Tell me what to do Rhoda, and I'll do it. You know I'm on your side. But fire him? What will he do? Where will he work? I'll tell you what—I'll talk to him, and if it ever happens again he's out."

It might have ended there, given Belkin's gentle touch, but that night Rhoda told the story to her boyfriend and the boyfriend suggested that she call the union.

The union agent, Kramer, was in the shop at eight o'clock the next morning, and the minor incident had blown into full-scale war.

It is the job of a union agent to protect and defend his workers, and in this sense Kramer was doing his job. He heard Rhoda's complaint, rounded up six sympathetic operators, and came marching into Belkin's office.

There were twenty-four other women who didn't see it that way. One of them had even mentioned to Kramer that the boy was backward and maybe he hadn't meant anything. Twenty-three others nodded in agreement, but they were the quiet ones. No one could stand up and say that Rhoda was wrong. It was a question of honor.

It is also important to understand that Kramer had to defend the honor. What is a union agent unless he responds to the complaint of a worker? Indeed, often he knows that the complaint is unjust but he must still respond. And he must *show* everyone that he is responding. He must carry the banner so that the people know the union is behind them; the union is their defender.

It would have been a good thing if Kramer had understood about Otto. After all, Otto had been there three years and he hadn't molested anyone. The situation was not black and white. And goodness knows Rhoda's virginity was still intact if it was intact in the first place. Maybe she *had* been pinched. That wasn't the issue. The issue was Otto: a kind, lovable man-child. The issue was: Do they fire him?

Even Kramer wouldn't have fired him if he had understood. But he had six wildcats urging him on a case that was sounding more like rape every minute. And don't think, just because Belkin and Sharnik were afraid of Kramer, that the operators were. These were women who battled sewing machines eight hours a day. If Kramer had backed down they would have chased him right down the fire escape.

So Kramer came into Belkin's office and told him that he would pull six operators off their jobs that minute unless the rapist was fired. Six operators off meant that the shop would close down at once because the flow of work was progressive, and if it could not get through certain key machines it could not move on to the next operator.

Belkin was frightened of course. He tried to argue, glossing over the whole thing, saying everything would be all right, suggesting that Kramer and Rhoda and he all go out to lunch and talk it over. Nothing would do. So Belkin rose from his desk and went to find Sharnik, to whom he was otherwise not talking.

Sharnik asked Kramer and Rhoda into his office and listened carefully to the complaint as though he were a judge in the Appellate Division.

"Where did he grab you, Rhoda? On the leg? That's not a crime. The law does not presume a man guilty of assault or sexual abuse because he pinches a woman on the leg. Besides, I've examined our union contract and I see nothing here that demands that I dismiss a longtime employee for the charges you are claiming. If you want to press charges with the police because someone pinched you, that is not my business."

There was that air of smugness as Sharnik finished. Rhoda was steaming. Even Kramer, who didn't give much of a damn about an idle indiscretion, was steaming.

"If there wasn't a lady present, Sharnik, I would tell you what you could do with your legal interpretations. But instead I am giving you two choices: Either you fire the boy this afternoon or I pull the shop on strike tomorrow. You can give me your answer tomorrow morning."

The shop went back to work and Belkin and Sharnik each sat alone in his office cursing each other for not handling the situation. As Sharnik saw it, a few martinis should have been enough to patch up the whole thing. As Belkin saw it, Sharnik should certainly have been able to find some clause in the labor contract that would resolve it.

At two o'clock Belkin walked into Sharnik's office and told him that they ought to talk about Otto. It was not a long discussion; they agreed at once that if it was between firing Otto and suffering a strike, it would be the former.

They both went back to their own offices and sat quietly, thinking about dismissing the awkward, retarded young man for a crime that they knew he had not committed. And as they thought about it, their shame grew stronger than their fright.

An hour later Sharnik shuffled into Belkin's office. He was almost in tears.

"I'll tell you what, Belkin," he said, "the choice is not whether I fire Otto or I suffer a strike. The choice for me is whether I can live with myself."

Belkin rose from his chair and gave Sharnik an enormous hug.

At ten o'clock the next morning Kramer sat with the two partners.

"Well, what will it be?" he asked.

"We don't want a strike, Kramer," Sharnik answered. "A strike will not only shut us down, it will put us out of business. We are a small company. If we cannot ship our orders the stores will have plenty of other companies to buy from. The result of a strike is that we lose our company and thirty women lose their jobs."

"So you agree to fire the boy," Kramer said.

"Let me tell you about the boy," said Belkin. "You know he's unfortunate, you know he's retarded. He has been here for three years. He sweeps the floor. The buyer from Woolworth comes up, he runs down and gets her coffee. This is maybe the only shop in New York that will hire him, and that is only because we already have him. I could fire him, Kramer; I lose nothing in firing him, except self-respect..."

"Would *you* fire him, Kramer?" Sharnik interjected. "After all, you're a wise man. You have visited many shops and listened to many complaints. Would you fire a defective young man for pinching an operator? For a one-time indiscretion that maybe he didn't even do? Isn't it possible that his hand brushed against her thigh and that was all there was to it?"

"The girl has made a formal complaint, gentlemen. There is nothing else to consider."

"How about considering what's right and what's wrong?"

"You have to give me your answer, gentlemen. I have a job to do."

No one spoke for about a minute and then Belkin said, "Sharnik and I have talked this over. We will not fire the boy. Furthermore we want to bring this matter to Dobrin, the president of the union. Everyone knows Dobrin is fair-minded in a matter like this."

"You can't take it to Dobrin. It is not a matter for Dobrin."

"I *can* take it to Dobrin, and the way to do it is simply to lift up this damn telephone and get him on the end of it. There is a boy's future at stake here. We're not talking about pajamas. I'll get Dobrin on the phone and tell him the story. I'll tell him that I have to fire a boy who's mentally defective because some operator says he pinched her. I'll tell him that you're here and you're threatening a strike unless I fire the kid. I'll tell him that—and then goddammit you can tell him your side of it."

"And what if Dobrin agrees with me?" Kramer said.

"Then I have to tell you with some regret that before I am forced to fire this boy I am going to call the *New York Post* and tell them the story. You can push us around, Kramer, with our little pajama business, but you can't push around the newspapers. So before you strike us, make sure the union is ready to have this story on page four."

Belkin, in his whole life, had never talked that way. Sharnik smiled quietly and wished he could tell him how much he admired him.

Kramer lit a cigar and puffed it quietly. Then he took a little yellow pill out of his vest pocket and swallowed it with some coffee.

"You know, I've got six hotheads on my back. They expect to see the kid fired."

"And I've got twenty-four *ladies* who would cry to see it happen," said Sharnik. "Twenty-four ladies who I have to face every morning, who I live with eight hours a day. If I fire the kid I might as well not show up in the morning."

Kramer reached into his pocket and pulled out a peppermint Life Saver. "What do I tell Rhoda and the six wildcats?" he asked.

It was a good question, but Sharnik had the answer. He had already considered that it might come down to this and that Kramer would need a face-saving approach.

"We tell the people," he said, "that we are all very much disturbed by the incident and that we cannot agree what is to be done. We also tell them that we do not want to fire someone without a proper investigation, especially a boy like Otto. We tell them that we are taking the whole matter to arbitration and that we will let an impartial arbitrator decide."

"And what do we do after he decides?"

Belkin was standing and he placed his arm on Kramer's shoulder. "You're not such a bad guy, Kramer. You're a very understanding and sensitive man. What we do is take our time about the arbitration and let the tempers cool. If anyone asks, we say that we are waiting for the arbitration to be scheduled. In a month Rhoda won't want to go to arbitration. You'll tell her that arbitration could be a bother. I'll have one of the girls talk to her in a few weeks and point out that Otto is really a gentle soul, and doesn't she want to give him another chance. All in all we'll never get to arbitration."

There was a two-inch ash on Kramer's cigar. He nodded his head quietly. "If the kid pinches one more behind, you promise to dismiss him right then and there, correct?"

And the case of Otto, and whatever the hell he did, came to an end.

Kramer wrapped up his notes and walked out into the shop to tell everyone what he had agreed to. Naturally he made himself the hero, which is the way these things have to be resolved.

Belkin and Sharnik sat together in the office, exhausted, and just at that moment the Woolworth buyer walked into the showroom. "What a time," thought Belkin. "When I *want* her I can never get her." But he straightened his tie, put on his best smile, and went out to say hello.

The Man Who
Wanted to Buy a Heart

When Reuben wanted to buy a heart he went downtown to see Markowitz, who dealt in all commodities.

"I can buy you many things," said Markowitz, "but not a heart. A heart is not for sale."

"They told me that Markowitz can buy anything," said Reuben.

"Markowitz can buy anything, but Markowitz cannot buy the sun. And Markowitz cannot buy a heart."

"I must have a heart," said Reuben.

For generations it was known that if you wanted something very badly and could pay the price, you went to see Markowitz. Markowitz never disappointed. Nor had his father nor grandfather in the old country. From all over, people came to see Markowitz, and he always delivered.

So perhaps it was not surprising that Markowitz went around to see who would sell his heart.

He first approached Dworkin, the butcher, about whom it was said that everything had a price.

"You want to buy my heart?" said Dworkin. "What are you offering?"

"A million dollars, Dworkin—it's not a bad price. I came to you first, as a friend, that you should have first opportunity. For a million dollars I could go to Kessler's son, who races bicycles."

Dworkin knew enough not to show any sign of interest, but told Markowitz to come back tomorrow.

But tomorrow, Dworkin didn't want to sell his heart.

So Markowitz went to Zimmerman, the cutter.

"Good day, Zimmerman."

"What's good?"

"I bring you a proposition that could cheer you up. I have a client who is looking for something and he is willing to pay a large price."

"What's large?"

"A million dollars," said Markowitz.

"Hah! For a million dollars he can buy my heart," said Zimmerman.

"That is what he wants to buy," said Markowitz.

Zimmerman sat down. When Markowitz was looking for something he did not joke.

But for all Zimmerman's troubles, he would not sell his heart. So Markowitz thanked him and went on his way.

Nor was Markowitz successful anywhere else in finding a heart for Reuben.

Three times Reuben called on him to ask how he was progressing, and three times Markowitz had to admit that so far he could not provide.

He was most upset about it. In his whole life he never had a request he could not deliver. It was known in the whole community.

So upset was Markowitz that he suffered long periods of depression and inability to work. He had no joy in finding things and turned down all requests and offers. He could neither deliver Reuben's request, nor admit to Reuben that he couldn't deliver.

And so, one day, when Reuben came to ask how Markowitz was doing, Markowitz said, "I have found what you want, Reuben. I have found you a heart."

"Could I meet my heart?" asked Reuben, not meaning a joke.

Markowitz held out his hand. "You have just met him; it is my own heart that I will sell."

Reuben was stunned and about to protest, but he thought better of it. It was no time for courtesies.

"Tomorrow we will go to the doctor and he will listen to your heart, Markowitz, and if it is sound we have a deal."

"A million dollars," said Markowitz.

"That's the price," said Reuben.

How strange a man was Markowitz. He slept well that night and smiled to himself that for a hundred years no Markowitz had failed to deliver.

The following day he met Reuben at the doctor.

For a million dollars Reuben was entitled to security, and Markowitz went through an extensive physical examination. He was in his sixties, smoked two packs a day, but was otherwise in good health.

And when the examination was completed and Reuben and Markowitz were in the doctor's office, the doctor confirmed that Markowitz's heart was sound.

"However, please understand that 'sound' does not mean first class. It is an old man's heart. If I were rating hearts I would have to say it's second-rate."

Little it mattered to Markowitz whether they buried him without a second-rate heart or without a first-rate heart. But Reuben was thinking carefully.

And when they left the office and walked on to the street, Reuben said to Markowitz, "The doctor says your heart is second-rate."

"You asked me, Reuben, to find you a heart. A rating chart you didn't give me."

"Still, it is not first-quality."

"I have found you a heart," said Markowitz, "whether or not you buy it is up to you."

"No…it isn't that…I need a heart. But a million dollars is too much for a second-rate heart."

"You want to offer me a lower price for my heart?" said Markowitz in disbelief.

"A half-million would be fair," said Reuben. "I could go maybe another hundred thousand."

"That's tops, then?" asked Markowitz.

Reuben nodded and they walked quietly for a few blocks.

They walked around the neighborhood, by Krinsky's Appetizers and Chodosh's newsstand. By Dworkin's butcher shop, where Markowitz waved. And by A.B.C. Lingerie, where Zimmerman was cutting on the ninth floor.

It was a nice day, getting nicer, thought Markowitz.

Finally Reuben turned to him. "I've thought it over. I would go to three-quarters of a million," he said.

Markowitz just smiled.

They walked a few more blocks and Markowitz said goodbye. And he never saw Reuben again.

And it continued to be known that if you wanted something very badly and could pay the price, you went to see Markowitz and he would always deliver.

A Gentleman From
Sole to Crown

It was the day of the bra order that he first noticed her. She fluttered into his office, "We need more size 36 bras, B cup," she said.

"Ahem," he said, or something like that.

"The pink and blue style with the lace edge…"

"Mrs. McCarthy orders those things," he said.

"Oh, I'm sorry…I thought…"

She turned toward the door and he watched the twist of her skirt ride up her thigh, and she was gone.

Nobody charged into his office. People knocked quietly, tiptoed in, waited to be spoken to. Perhaps it was his dress: dark suit and vest, always. A white shirt—men had started to wear pale blue and beige—he wore white, collar held down with a silver clip.

Perhaps it was his countenance: quiet, thoughtful, deeply intelligent; cynical, impatient, intolerant. He was the wrong man to bring a problem that hadn't been evaluated.

"The Johnstown Dungaree Company is raising our price two dollars a pair," said his head buyer. "I'm not going to pay it."

"Then you have someone else in mind to get the dungarees from?" And the buyer would redden, regretting his haste, resenting the answer.

The personnel said he was iron-willed, rigid and forbidding. Everyone but Marsha.

She had only worked in the store six months; a stock girl, an assistant buyer to stretch a point. She hummed around the store like a bumblebee, folding stock, climbing the ladders to help a customer, shouting down from the top rung, "Mrs. McCarthy, we're out of panties—size 14—tea rose!" In those days panties were something you didn't shout about.

He heard it also—about the panties—but it didn't penetrate. He was insulated from small talk, from petty arguments, from everyday things. He lived in that cloister of himself, with an armed guard at every entrance.

Which was why it stunned him when she told him about the bras. Thirty-six B, for godsakes. Wasn't she embarrassed—a young woman of twenty-eight—to be telling him about bra sizes?

After that he noticed her, appeared not to notice her, but noticed her, and casually wandered to where she was counting stock. "The bras haven't come in yet," she said. "I had two women here this morning." She looked up at him. "Oh, I'm sorry..."

The truth was that he liked to hear her talk about it. It unnerved him, frightened him a bit, but he liked it. It wasn't the bras; it wasn't the intimacy. It was that she could talk that way.

He also liked to hear her curse; not vulgar, but pretty good barroom stuff, a healthy streak of goddamns and hells strung together.

And she was attractive.

She buzzed around the shop, perpetual motion, mumbling, whistling, cursing; where are the goddamn dungarees? And always sucking on the honey drops which she lifted by the handful out of the penny barrel.

He knew he was in trouble the day he found a honey drop right in the center of his desk. Arrogant, he thought. Presumptuous. But he smiled.

"Thought you'd like one," she tossed off, and she turned to him, not flirting, not seductive, not anything, and looked up at him with very wide-open green eyes.

"It's impossible," he thought. "I'm forty-seven and married. She's twenty-eight and married." But he knew it was not impossible.

From that moment she was always with him. When she was away, her shadow was with him. She hung on him like a problem he couldn't solve, like a worry he couldn't shed. He didn't even want her there, always on the edge of his consciousness, but she was there.

And in the store she was a magnet, and he would find some excuse to check the stock where she was standing, to touch her arm ever so lightly, and yet to touch her arm. A schoolboy would have acted more mature; he knew it.

He wasn't sure what anything meant. Nothing like this had ever happened before. There were no boundary lines, no rules, no precedents. His whole life was precedents.

It was impossible, wasn't it, that he could love her? He liked her—yes, that was it—he was attracted to her. My god, even *he* could be attracted to a lovely shape, couldn't he? Couldn't he?

It was on the evening of December 31st, inventory day, that they were alone in the store. Mrs. McCarthy would have been there, but she was ill. The first inventory Mrs. McCarthy had missed in seventeen years. The stock boys had gone home; it was, after all, New Year's Eve.

"You can go ahead, Marsha; it's seven o'clock. I can finish."

"I thought I could help you," she said. "My husband and I never celebrate New Year's Eve anyway. I told him it was inventory time and that I'd be home very late."

There was a rush of electricity through his body. His face became warm. He was a bit startled and he had to catch his breath.

"Well then at least I owe you dinner. Shall we go out for an hour and finish later? Can you wait outside just a moment while I change my shirt?"

"I could sit here and talk to you," she whispered. "I won't be embarrassed."

He felt the power and control seep out of him. He thought about changing his shirt in front of another woman—an employee actually—it was unheard of. He thought about how he might do it. Should he turn away from her? Could he do it all without loosening his belt?

And what if she told? What if she told one of the stockboys? Or Mrs. McCarthy?

He turned toward her, caught the incredible green eyes and held them. And then he slowly pulled off his tie and started to unbutton the front of his shirt. He was on fire, and yet it wasn't lust. It was in his face and chest, and his heart pounded.

"Wouldn't you like to step outside now?" he said.

"Not if you're only going to change your shirt."

He loosened his belt, separating the tongue and the buckle. Then he opened the top button of the pants and pulled the zipper half way down. The front of the pants separated and he was able to lift out the shirt. He took the clean shirt from the desk behind him, and without even turning away from her, put it on, tucked it in, closed the zipper and tightened his belt.

"That was very difficult for you," she said.

He looked at her, and his eyes were wet. He took one step toward her and placed his hand on her shoulder, his thumb and forefinger touching the softness of her neck.

"You don't have to be so tight," she said at dinner. "Nothing has happened. This isn't anything. You could try to see it that way."

But it wasn't nothing. It was something. And whether she could see that or not hardly changed anything.

Yet, what was it? Had he touched her? Had he even tried to kiss her? What had he done except to change his shirt? It was good for him, actually. He could almost make that argument. It forced him out of his fortress. It forced him to venture. He thought of what Kierkegaard had said, "To venture causes anxiety, but not to venture is to lose one's self."

"I'm not sure it's proper for us to be having dinner together," he said.

"I think you're probably allowed to take an employee out to dinner," she answered, "and if you need to justify it, you did say you owed me dinner. We've been working on inventory since eight this morning…"

"Yes…if someone saw us…I guess we could explain it that way."

"Do we have to explain it? What is it that we have to explain?"

He looked at her. Nobody spoke to him this way. Nobody challenged. Nobody contradicted. And nobody was ever right. She was right.

"You're right. I know you're right. But it doesn't feel right. I'm not sure that you understand how it was when I grew up."

"But you don't want it to be that way do you? You don't want it that way, and you—more than anyone I have ever met—can make it the way you want it. You have the force…I've never felt a force like you have."

She was right about the force, although he would have called it determination. People sensed it in him, deferred to him, admired him, respected him. It was almost an homage.

It was what he wanted…yes…but not all of what he wanted. He wanted to be free. He wanted to be out of the fortress. He wanted people to be able to touch him; and he wanted to touch. And most of all, most of anything, he wanted to be able to do what she insisted he do. He wanted to be able to change his shirt; to do it and not to have to torment himself.

When they returned to the store, hours had slipped by and it was past time for inventory. They took off their coats, made a feeble effort at gathering their papers, and then turned into each other's arms. He held her there, steadily, kissed her deeply on the mouth, and felt her lips part ever so slightly. That was all.

She left. He sat at his desk, chin cradled in his hands, and thought and thought about where he was and where he soon might be. And at that moment someone passed the window of his office and turned the key in the lock. He was startled for a moment, looked at his watch—it was eleven—time for the night watchman to arrive. He had known Martin for thirty-five years; had known him as a young boy when he had visited his father's store. Martin was now in his late seventies, not so much a watchman as just an old employee and an old friend.

Martin tapped lightly on his office door, entered, and stood there with his crumpled hat in his right hand. "Happy New Year, Martin," he said.

Martin just stood there, sort of shifting from foot to foot.

"Is there something you want, Martin?"

"I don't exactly know how to say this sir, and maybe I shouldn't, but it's many years sir, and I thought I would tell you—you see I was walking this way just before…and…well, sir, just be careful is all."

After work the following day she asked if she could speak with him privately.

"I have to give notice," she said. "We leave in three weeks for Arizona. George has asthma. We have to go."

"How long have you known?"

"A month, perhaps."

"And last night?"

"Last night was last night."

"What would have happened with us if you weren't going?"

"I don't know. What do you think?"

"I'm no good at talking about that. Why don't you tell me."

"I would have asked you to come to bed with me."

"Impossible. I'm forty-seven—you're twenty-eight."

"I can't help that," she said.

He wanted her then, desperately. He wanted to gather her up, to touch her. To hear her talk.

In three weeks she was gone.

The night after, he was in his office late, thinking. On the opposite wall hung the portrait of his grandfather, the founder; next to that a photograph of his father. To his left, a fire axe hung on the wall, and somehow his eyes attached themselves to it. Finally he rose from his chair, removed the axe from the wall, and walked out on the floor. Towering over one of the wooden counters, he raised the axe over his head the full length of his reach and brought it down with all his might, splitting the counter in half, scattering the lingerie, and burying the blade deep in the wooden floor.

Kessler and the
Grand Scheme

In the old days of the garment center, if you walked into Dubrow's Cafeteria on Seventh Avenue for your morning coffee, you would enter a world of cutters, pressers, and patternmakers, all unemployed or laid off. You would hear the stories of the discontented: the bosses are unreasonable, the unions are corrupt, the buyers are compromised. They would say, if they were in charge, things would be different. It is the language of Seventh Avenue; everyone thinks he should be running General Motors. And so it should not surprise you that one morning they told the story of Kessler and his grand scheme.

Kessler, a man of failed opportunities, was one day reading the obituaries in *The New York Times* when he came upon the name Morris Pearlstein. "My god, I knew him," Kessler said to himself. "He worked next to me as a presser in the old pajama factory on 29th Street."

Kessler had been part of the New York apparel world before it moved to Georgia and South Carolina and then to China, working as a cutter, a presser, sometimes doing a little shipping, and never holding a job for more than a year or two. Companies found him difficult, always quarreling, always negative, and since pressers were not scarce in the marketplace, the companies did not have to put up with him and he was soon out the door. He never held a job long enough to save any money, and so, aside from being difficult, Kessler was poor.

As he read Pearlstein's obituary the picture of Pearlstein returned to his mind, and what he remembered most was that Pearlstein, for a presser in a garment factory, was a very sharp dresser. Nobody in the old garment factories dressed very well because nobody was paid a living wage. And besides, the factories were full of fabric shavings and dripping machine oil.

So Kessler thought back to his days working next to Pearlstein and admiring Pearlstein's attire, and he thought, wouldn't it have been nice if Pearlstein had left him one of his stylish suits.

Kessler thought about this for a while when he was struck by an idea: What is Mrs. Pearlstein going to do with the suits anyway? So he leafed through the phone book, got a number, and called Mrs. Pearlstein, a woman he had never met.

"Mrs. Pearlstein, I called to express my sympathies. Morris and I were old friends from the garment factory—a very fine man. We worked side by side in the pressing area and spent many hours talking about our jobs and our families. We were very close, like brothers. I remember especially how well Morris dressed—how stylish were his suits and ties."

"Well, it is very thoughtful of you to call, Mr. Kessler. My memory is no longer so good, but I do remember Morris mentioning you."

"You could call me Irving," said Kessler. "You know, Morris and I had a little joke. I admired his suits, especially the navy blue, and Morris said, if he died he would will it to me. Of course, it was just a little thing between us, but I wonder, Mrs. Pearlstein, now that Morris has gone to a better place, whether you have any use for the suit. It would be an honor to own something of Mr. Pearlstein's."

"The suit—what do I need it for? It goes anyway to the Salvation Army. Come by and pick it up."

And so, in a few days, Pearlstein's navy blue suit hung in Kessler's closet. Indeed, an interesting idea had entered Kessler's otherwise inactive mind. The following week he scanned the obituaries again, and although there was no one he knew, he found the name of a man about his age who had worked in the garment center. It took a little courage, but he was soon on the phone with Mrs. Greenberg.

"You don't know me, Mrs. Greenberg, but I called to express my condolences. Mr. Greenberg and I were friends from the garment center, and I was just wondering…"

"A suit? You want a suit?" said Mrs. Greenberg, a bit bewildered. "Well, what am I going to do with them anyway? Come, you can have two suits."

So Kessler's closet was soon full, and the rest of his apartment resembled the men's wear racks in Filene's Basement. Of course, many of the suits were not in Kessler's size, but that hardly mattered because Kessler had connected with a closeout shop on the lower East Side, which happily paid him forty or fifty dollars for a suit. Kessler, late in his life, had become an entrepreneur.

In time, Kessler's bravado exceeded all limits. At the beginning he had held his conversation to a few words, just enough to get the suits, but with experience, he grew confident, anticipating the questions. He became so adept that he now accepted invitations to have a cup of tea and chat about the old times.

"Well no, Mrs. Brodsky, we didn't work side by side; we were in different parts of the factory, but we occasionally had coffee and talked about the trials of the working class."

Or, "No, we were not the same size, but he didn't promise the suit to me. You see, I had a cousin who fell on hard times..."

He could handle everything and the grieving widow was often happy for a little company.

And anyway, the widows thought, why would anyone lie about this? Who would invent such a story?

Time marched on and Kessler was doing very nicely. He made his weekly visit to the shop on Orchard Street and pocketed his fifty dollars when a most unexpected event occurred. Standing behind him at the counter of the shop one day were two ladies, friends, it turned out.

"Why Mr. Kessler, how nice to see you again, but aren't you carrying the very suit I gave you last Tuesday?"

To which the other lady said, "You know Mr. Kessler?"

The jig was up. The gun was smoking.

"So would you rather," said the first lady, "that I call the police or that I send the Salvation Army around tomorrow morning? And I will naturally expect an appropriate check to The Hebrew Retirement Home in honor of your dear friend and co-worker whose suit you are about to exchange for fifty dollars."

***

Alas, it is somehow the law of the garment center that the grand schemes, however imaginative, inevitably fail. Like a feudal manor, the lords remain lords and the serfs remain serfs. And so Kessler, inventor of a grand scheme and on his way to join the world of entrepreneurs, is back at Dubrow's Cafeteria telling his story to nods of approval, but finally back to where he started.

THE TWENTY-NINE PENS
OF SIMON ENGLEHART

"To my three children, all worthless, I leave my fortune, of equal value. My body, such as it is, I leave to science. To the Garment Industry Association I leave nothing. It has given me nothing so we are even. Only to Grossman do I leave something of value, my collection of pens."

Thus read the last will and testament of Simon Englehart, who departed from Seventh Avenue and rose to heaven at the age of seventy-three.

I am thus the inheritor of twenty-nine pens which I keep in a cigar box lined with red flannel. There is an old Waterman fountain pen in a tortoise-shell casing, and a 19¢ Bic ballpoint. There's a black Flair felt-tip and a pen that writes in four colors, depending on which point you press through the opening. Englehart spent ten years collecting pens, the total value of which might be $29.00.

I hired Englehart twenty years ago. He applied for a salesman's job and I knew at once he was too old. He wore a double-breasted suit with a red carnation and he carried a walking stick with a fake diamond imbedded in the handle large enough to guide lost ships to shore.

"You are thinking, Grossman, that I am too old for this job. You are thinking why not get a young man who can run around the market and do a little shopping in the afternoons. You are forgetting what Shakespeare and Wordsworth said about the poetry of age. You are forgetting about style, grace and nobility."

He rapped the cane once or twice on the edge of my desk, the diamond blinking at me, and I observed that I could hang that cut crystal in the showroom to replace part of the chandelier.

I hired him. I knew it was a mistake when I did it but I did it. I think I might have been hypnotized. I think he waved the cane back and forth enough times to put me under.

We manufactured children's pajamas, a small forty-machine shop on 36th Street trying to slug it out in the world's toughest marketplace. Maybe selling encyclopedias is harder but not much harder. You get to work before eight and hurry to one of the buying offices where there are already seventeen salesmen in front of you. You hand your card to the receptionist who sits behind a glass shield that's cracked and mended with Scotch tape turned the color of old bourbon. The magazines are *Field and Stream* and *National Geographic,* some of the issues from last year, others with pages torn out, presumably by salesmen who dreamed of someday taking a vacation in Bali or Honolulu. A pin-up calendar hangs on the wall turned to August; it's October. Someone has pencilled a circle around a predictable part of the anatomy. It has been erased, but not very well. Another salesman wanders over and asks how's business. You tell him terrible. You always say terrible because if you say not bad he rushes to the stores, buys all your styles and copies them. Into such a jungle did I send Englehart, the poet.

Did I first train him? Did I first introduce him to the fabrics and the trimmings? Did I even tell him about the idiosyncrasies of some of the buyers? Of course not; that's not what happens in the garment center. In other industries there are training programs and apprenticeships even for experienced salesmen. In the garment center we give a man the sample line on the second day and tell him, "Don't come back without an order!" Some old-timers send them out the first day.

On the second day Englehart arrived at work with a copy of *The Atlantic Monthly*. "They only have *National Geographic* in the waiting rooms," he said. I took the magazine and threw it in the wastebasket. "The buyer you're going to see didn't get past the seventh grade. Carry the *Daily News*," I said.

I don't know why I did it. I'm not that stupid. You don't change a salesman; his style is his style. Some buyers will like him, some buyers won't like him, and to some buyers you could send the line with a Saint Bernard; the salesman is faceless. Who knows, maybe some buyers read *The Atlantic*; maybe some buyers think a walking stick with the Hope Diamond is classy.

I guess I can't help the "seventh-grade" routine. There's a jock mentality in the garment center, not unlike a locker room. We think *survival of the fittest*. We think you sweat it out, fight for every edge. Education? We don't acknowledge education. Shakespeare and Wordsworth? What has that to do with selling pajamas? Underneath, we know. Underneath, some manufacturers can quote more Shakespeare than an English major at Amherst. But we don't let on. It comes I think from generations of pushcart peddlers who got up with the sun and struggled for every nickel. Hard work was all they knew. We follow that tradition.

But I'm drifting…I know it. Back to Englehart and the fountain pens.

After three weeks Englehart hadn't sold many pajamas but I will admit it was fun when he returned from the marketplace. He would come into my office and tell me which buyer he saw, breaking into a marvelous imitation of the buyer's voice and mannerisms. He could do them all, the women and the men. He knew I loved it and he kept it up as long as he could, until finally I asked about *the paper*.

The paper? That means the order; the written order, not the promised order. In the whole history of the garment center salesmen have been coming back to the office with promises of how many dozen the buyer is going to write, and most of the time there is some discrepancy between promise and delivery. So there has evolved an understanding: You don't talk about it unless it's on paper. WHERE'S THE PAPER? has become the time-honored cry of 7th Avenue.

Well of course Englehart never had the paper, although the recital of his expectations was the most imaginative I have ever heard. But one tires of expectations, even delivered with a bit of soft-shoe, and one day I got kind of annoyed.

"Englehart, cut out the song-and-dance and bring back some orders. Where the hell were you all morning, in the coffee shop? Woolworth?...you claim you were at Woolworth and you don't even bring back a sample order? I don't believe you were at Woolworth!"

Maybe that wasn't the nicest thing to say. Your word matters in the garment center. Whatever else may be said, a person's word counts. A little window-dressing is O.K. A little fanciful expectation is O.K. But if you say you're at Woolworth, you're at Woolworth.

Englehart stiffened and then turned and walked out of the office. I had made another mistake, a bad one.

The following week I forgot the whole thing and when Englehart returned from the market I asked him where he had been. "Woolworth," he said.

"Woolworth? What are you having an affair with the buyer? Where's the goddamn paper?"

"No paper," said Englehart.

"No paper? Christ! I don't know where the hell you go in the mornings, Englehart."

"Woolworth," he said again, quietly, and then he reached into his inside breast pocket, pulled out a fountain pen and laid it on my desk.

"What's that?" I asked.

"That's Mary Callahan's fountain pen. I stole it from her desk this morning when she wasn't looking."

I looked up slowly at Englehart. His lips were tight, his face pale. He was a little shaken. No imitations, no routine. Just the buyer's fountain pen sitting on the desk in front of me.

Over the next few years Englehart didn't get any better. The buyers didn't like him very much. He had a way of showing the line that sounded condescending. Like he was saying, "What am I, Englehart, lover of fine arts and poetry, doing selling flannel pajamas?"

And he had a way of getting poetry into the sales pitch. "Look at this print—daffodils—exquisite! Do you know what Wordsworth wrote about a field of daffodils?"

The buyer would look at him and shake his head slightly. "The price, Englehart. Just tell me the price!"

So there wasn't much paper and more than once I was on the verge of firing him. But at that moment, somehow, Englehart would reach into his pocket and bring out a pen.

"Betty Clark's pen. I lifted it off her desk this morning. You don't believe me? I'll call her right now; you can listen on the other line. I'll tell her there's an extra pen among my things and ask if it's hers."

It happened about every six months, after a dry spell. He just sensed when I would begin to question, or at least to wonder, where he had been. Nothing more, nothing said. It became a little understanding between us.

Actually there was something said. Englehart had a curious way of keeping track of the pen collection. He tallied how many miles all the pens would write. Some information came from the advertising but in other cases he wrote the pen companies. If I asked about the collection he would say, "I've got eighteen hundred miles," as though he were taking a long trip.

One day he brought back two pens. By now, ten years had passed and there were twenty-seven pens in my bottom drawer. Twenty-seven pens and not a word about any one of them except whose desk it came from and how many miles it would write.

"This morning I was at Kmart—Frances Pomerantz—and I'm showing her the line. Frances is fighting to stay awake and not hiding it in any way. Next desk over is a new assistant who Frances introduces as Greta something-or-other. Greta is wide awake and commenting on every garment I hang, most of her comments being that my price is too high."

"Englehart, didn't we see that style last season? Aren't you going to show us anything new?

"Englehart, you're at least two dollars higher than any other manufacturer on that style. Sleepytime has it in their line for $22.50."

"Mind you," says Englehart, "this is coming from an assistant buyer who might be twenty-two years old and can't tell nylon from polyester.

"Anyway, Greta and I are glaring at each other when Frances says that Greta will soon be taking over the department because Frances is being moved to sheets and linens.

"I look at Greta and smile, and Greta gives me a look which says—I don't think I can repeat in civilized surroundings what it says—and that moment both Frances and Greta leave the room because their merchandise manager is calling. I figure things are going to be pretty sparse around here for another decade and so I begin to scan Frances's desk and immediately notice a lovely tortoise-shell Waterman, vintage 1940, or anyway pre-war. Of course I snatch it and I hardly have it tucked away when I notice on Greta's desk a solid-red Esterbrook. I have no use for the Esterbrook because the Waterman will do the job nicely. But I figure if Greta is writing with an Esterbrook instead of a 19¢ Bic ballpoint she must be very fond of it. So I snatch that also."

"That brings us up to twenty-nine pens," I said. But I couldn't help thinking this time was unique. Two pens stolen; we were moving from symbolic gesture to grand larceny. The next time he could clear out every pen in the building.

But the next time never came.

Three days later Englehart came into my office and said he was retiring.

I asked why he was retiring. Was it his age? I told him we could arrange something a little easier. He had, after all, worked for the company for twenty years.

It wasn't age.

"Tell me what it is," I urged. "Did I do something wrong? Is it money? Is it the rat race?"

He stood there a while and I guessed that he was considering whether he wanted to talk about it. Finally he said, "It was the twenty-ninth pen." That's all he said.

A week later we had a little retirement party for Englehart in my office; a cake, a few bottles of Four Roses, jokes and well wishes, and then everyone went home. Englehart and I stayed, and I took out the cigar box and we talked and laughed about the twenty-nine pens. The names tumbled forth—Mary Callahan, Betty Clark, Frances Pomerantz—and Englehart warmed up to his routine and did his little soft-shoe, tucking his walking stick under his arm.

"I lifted Betty Clark's pen right before her eyes. I remember that day, about seven years ago. I hadn't brought back an order in two weeks and I knew you were getting annoyed. I knew you would start in with your, "Where have you been?" speech and I knew it was time to bring back a pen. Betty had a simple Paper Mate ballpoint on her desk but the thing that got me excited was that it wrote in green ink. Betty wouldn't leave her desk or turn around and I knew I must have that pen. Finally I took our style 2985 tricot gown and I draped it right over her desk. "This is the hottest style in our whole line," I said.

"Get that goddamn rag off my desk. What's the matter with you!" she hollered.

"Holding the hanger in my left hand I swung my right hand under the garment and felt around for the pen. I had it in a moment and with a grand flourish I lifted the gown off her desk and presto-chango, the pen was gone."

We drank a toast to Betty Clark and Englehart did a quick two-liner in her high squeaky voice.

Indeed each pen had a story and each story had a little pain, a little joy, and often a little magic.

I handed him the cigar box and we said good-bye, and over the next ten years I spoke to him only occasionally. A month ago I heard that he had passed away and shortly after that the cigar box with the twenty-nine pens arrived at my office by private messenger.

I put the box back in the lower drawer where it had always been, and now and then I open it, look at the pens and think of Englehart. There is something touching, something poetic about what he did, and something terribly wise in knowing how many miles to go before the road came to an end.

THE MILLION DOLLAR
PROPOSITION

In Aaronson turned at once to his book of charts and graphs, flipping pages until he came to one headed IBM. His face turned white and his heartbeat quickened. There could be no question; the formula fed out by the computer, applied to the price of IBM stock on any given day, predicted whether the stock, exactly one week later, would rise or fall.

"Probably a fluke," thought Aaronson. "Maybe it just works for this month. I'd better try it over a longer period."

And for the next hour Aaronson pitted the formula against IBM stock prices over the past year, then over random dates three years ago, then ten years ago. His left eye began twitching and his undershirt dampened. He pulled the tape out of the machine and immediately made three copies, sliding the first behind a slit in the wallpaper, taping the second inside a can of Maxwell House drip that was almost empty, and slipping the third inside page 267 of *Moby Dick*. By now he was feverish and dizzy with excitement, and lay in his bed staring at the ceiling.

It was his hobby, the stock market. He had charted it and taped it, juggled it and conjured it, for thirty years. Now and then he bought twenty shares from his friend Krasnov, the broker. When he bought it, the stock went down. When he sold it, the stock went up. Sometimes he listened to Krasnov, but Krasnov was always wrong, except when he didn't listen to him; then Krasnov was always right. Nor was Krasnov kind to his twenty-share customer and old friend.

"So Aaronson?—I told you to buy Polaroid, didn't I? Did you listen to me? Did you have any faith? What you did was tell me about some graphs and numbers. Meanwhile, in the middle of your arithmetic, the stock went up ten points."

"But what about Texaco, Krasnov? Did you tell me to buy Texaco? Something about offshore drilling in the Gulf Stream. Did I buy twenty shares of Texaco? And what happened?"

"Listen, Aaronson, no broker is a hundred percent right. On the important moves you didn't listen. If you think you can get better advice for your twenty shares and your six phone calls every day, go ahead."

Aaronson lay in bed thinking about the conversations. Krasnov was right. Aaronson did call him six times a day. Before he bought a stock he wanted to know everything. He wanted the ratio of assets to liabilities; he wanted the gross profit percentage; he wanted the price/earnings ratio. Aaronson understood all these figures and he was a very cautious man. Even when he was ready to buy he would call Krasnov one more time to check current and fixed assets.

"What do I know about fixed assets!" hollered Krasnov. "The stock is going up. They just discovered a new oil field near Mobile. I got this straight from my Aunt Mildred who used to date the controller. When the word gets out this stock is going through the ceiling. You want to know about fixed assets? Maybe you want to know what the sales manager eats for breakfast every day."

Krasnov took a certain delight in abusing Aaronson. Hardly a stockbroker with any significant following, he exploded his frustrations on his old friend who would neither fight back nor take his business elsewhere.

All of this Aaronson thought about because all of this was about to change. Now he could buy in hundred share lots— actually thousand share lots. Maybe he would throw Krasnov a hundred shares now and then. He could amass millions of dollars—tens of millions. He had invented an infallible method for making money.

Maybe *The Wall Street Journal* would send a team to interview him. Maybe *The Times Financial* or *Forbes*. He played over the interview on his mental tape...

"We understand, Mr. Aaronson, (He liked *Mr.* Aaronson; everyone always called him Aaronson.) that you have developed a calculation that will forecast the movement of a given stock without a failure."

"Well, gentlemen..."

"You realize that this is unheard of in the history of the stock market and that its application could influence the entire world economy. A foreign nation, in possession of this formula, could accumulate most of the world's wealth. Could you smile once for a photo, Mr. Aaronson? This could be the cover of *Time* magazine."

An hour drifted by as Aaronson considered the cover of *Time* magazine. Maybe a small write-up on page twenty-seven would be better, he thought. He daydreamed about clipping out the column and sending it to Krasnov.

He thought about going into Paul Stuart and buying a shirt with French cuffs. A sixty-dollar tie, maybe.

Sleep captured the world-famous financier at 5:00 A.M. He awoke at 7:30 and ran a fast calculation on IBM. It showed the stock up 11 points at this time next week.

At 8:15 he took the F train to work, and at ten o'clock he called Krasnov from his desk.

"Hello Krasnov, what do you think about buying twenty shares of IBM at the market?"

"Is that a buy order, Aaronson, or is this a discussion? I'd like to know because I have four customers waiting on the other lines."

"It's a buy order, Krasnov. Put it in."

"I can't put it in, Aaronson, it's only your first phone call. I'll put it in in the afternoon after you find out how many words a minute can be typed on the new IBM Electric by the valedictorian at Katherine Gibbs Secretarial School."

Krasnov hung up and Aaronson was left there holding the phone. He waited until twelve to call Krasnov again. Meanwhile IBM went up seven points. It still had four more points to go, so at twelve o'clock he told Krasnov to buy.

"Listen Aaronson, I'll buy the stock, but it's up seven points in two hours. Maybe we should wait for it to back off a little. I wish I could tell when you're serious about buying a stock; we could have made seven points."

There was a lot in what Krasnov said. The stock *was* up seven points. But the spread for the week was eleven points and Aaronson still wanted to buy. "How does the market look, Krasnov?" he asked.

"Do I know how the market looks, Aaronson? Tomorrow we could invade Nicaragua for all I know. This afternoon they could announce wage-price controls. Who can tell in this world? Russia is bankrupt. Argentina is bankrupt. And Mexico is almost bankrupt. You want me to tell you how the market looks?"

Aaronson hung up the phone and didn't buy IBM. In the afternoon it went up four more points to 115, and hung around 115 all week. Aaronson didn't own it but the formula at least had proved absolutely accurate.

One week later, Aaronson's calculator showed that in the next seven days IBM would go down nine points. That meant of course that he couldn't buy, but he could sell—he could sell short. The problem was that Aaronson had never sold short, and even though he knew how to do it, the thought frightened him. So he called Krasnov.

"Absolutely not!" yelled Krasnov. "What are you, a manipulator? Suddenly you're a financial wizard for twenty shares? As an old friend, Aaronson, I have to tell you that shorting the market is no place for you. You don't have the money for it and you don't have the temperament for it. You sell short at 115 and IBM goes up to 125, they'll cart you right off to the emergency room."

IBM did drop exactly nine points for the week and at the end of the week Aaronson got a call from Krasnov.

"Hey, Aaronson, what are you doing—playing with a Ouija board? You got a relative at IBM? You carrying on with the controller's wife? What do you know that I don't know, Aaronson? You called that stock exactly right for two weeks in a row. I think I may have to listen to you next time."

Aaronson thought about telling Krasnov about the calculator but somehow he couldn't do it. It wouldn't be any fun to do it. The thing to do with Krasnov would be to buy and sell the stock the right way a few times. That would wake him up. Already Krasnov was starting to show a little interest, Aaronson thought.

But he did want to tell someone about the calculator. Not the formula, but just the fact that he had a formula. He wanted someone smart, someone with a few bucks. Someone who would know how to handle this, maybe pool some money with him. It was, after all, a million dollar proposition.

His friend, Melchior, owned a ladies' sportswear business and spent his vacation gambling for big chips in Las Vegas. He really was wealthy and didn't mind spending. They had had dinner together exactly two years ago at the Palm, and the check came to $130 for two. Melchior signed for it and Aaronson handed him $65 exactly. It really pained him.

The dinner conversation had also pained him because Melchior spent the whole time talking about a large conglomerate which had just offered him three and a half million for his company. Melchior expounded upon both sides of the proposition: to sell or not to sell. That was about it for the evening.

Still, Melchior was the guy to call. He would know about things like this. So he got him on the phone.

"Now let me hear this again, Aaronson, you're telling me that you have a calculator that can forecast the price of IBM stock? So why are you telling me? Why don't you just go out and buy IBM and make about a hundred million and buy yourself half of Chicago?"

Aaronson hesitated. "Because I don't know my way around in a situation like this and I don't have enough money to invest. By the time I accumulate enough money somebody will figure out the system. I need someone a little sophisticated in the market."

"Listen Aaronson, I'm flattered that you think I'm a little sophisticated in the market, but I'll let you in on a secret. Last month I had a very sophisticated hot tip that came straight from the accountant's mouth. It cost me five grand in two and half weeks."

"Nevertheless, Melchior, I have a system…"

"A system, that's what I need, a system! There are three hundred guys with systems. Look at the financial section of *The New York Times*. One guy says subscribe to his system and you can't lose because the market is going up. The next guy says buy his system because the market is going down and you can make a million by selling short. One guy says buy gold. Another guy says sell gold. How come if these guys all know what to do they have to put ads in the paper for people to subscribe to their systems? Listen Aaronson, why don't you give me a call in a few months and tell me how your system is doing and we can talk about it then?"

"I have a better idea," said Aaronson. "Try the system one time and we'll see if it works. If it doesn't work we don't go ahead. You can't lose."

"O.K., Aaronson, tell you what. Give me your phone number and I'll call you tomorrow. I'm right in the middle of a gin game."

So Aaronson gave Melchior his phone number and that night he ran a new calculation on IBM so he would have the figures ready when Melchior called. The calculator ticked its familiar sounds and threw out an astounding number: IBM would be up seventeen points for the week.

Aaronson made a lot of notes because Melchior talked fast and Aaronson wanted to stay with him. The deal he would offer Melchior was fifty-fifty. Both of them would put up an equal amount of money and Melchior would do the buying and selling through his broker. Aaronson, of course, would make all the buy and sell decisions.

He was pleased with the arrangement. Melchior would manage the affair. He was used to giving orders. If his broker couldn't execute them fast enough he would find a different broker. And as soon as he had a few profitable trades he would realize that Aaronson's system was flawless and that they could ride it to incredible riches.

By three o'clock in the afternoon Melchior hadn't called. In a half hour the market would close. They had almost lost the day. Aaronson debated calling Melchior and two or three times he started to dial but he backed off. Probably Melchior was in the middle of a meeting with the conglomerate that was buying him out.

At 3:30 Aaronson could wait no longer. He dialed Top Flight Sportswear and asked for Melchior.

"Who's calling?" a pleasant voice asked.

"Just tell him Aaronson. It's a personal call."

"Just a minute, please," the voice put him on hold and some music started playing. Very high class. In a moment the operator returned.

"I'm terribly sorry. Mr. Melchior has left town and is not expected back until next week. I will leave word that you called."

"That's not possible!" Aaronson heard himself screaming. "Mr. Melchior is waiting for my call. He's expecting my call. Tell him again that Aaronson is on the phone. Aaronson. Remind him that it's about IBM stock."

The phone clicked and Aaronson stood there quietly. Finally he put it back on the receiver. There was sweat on the shiny black surface.

On the F train, at five-thirty, Aaronson turned to the back pages of the *New York Post*. The stock quotations weren't final but they were enough to tell what had happened to IBM that day. He turned the pages, holding his breath until he saw the financial headlines: STOCKS MIXED IN ACTIVE TRADING. Then he turned to IBM. Down a point, at 105. Nothing had happened. The 17-point rise hadn't started yet. He still had a chance tomorrow.

That night he ran the formula through the calculator a dozen times. And each time it threw out the result Aaronson grew more confident. To hell with Melchior, he thought. What did he need Melchior for. And to hell with Krasnov—he would give Krasnov the buy order and if Krasnov tried to talk him out of it he would find another broker.

The following day was one of those great historic days of the New York Stock Exchange. The *Times* would later read: DOW JONES AVERAGES UP 73 POINTS—HIGHEST RISE SINCE 1972.

Aaronson got to Krasnov before the market opened.

"Krasnov—place 20 shares of IBM at the market. We should get it around 105. Call me and confirm the price."

He hung up the phone and returned to work, content that he had started on a journey that could only make him wealthy and famous. At 11:00 he checked on the market. IBM was already up eight points. The averages were going wild. The market had already set an 11:00 record for the number of shares traded. *Everybody* was buying.

At 11:15 he called Krasnov to find out what price he had paid for the stock. The operator told him he would have to hold; Mr. Krasnov already had three calls waiting. He held for about five minutes when a voice broke through...

"Who are you waiting for please?"

"For Krasnov. I've been holding for five minutes."

"I'm terribly sorry. It's a little wild down here today. Mr. Krasnov has four calls waiting."

"He can't have four calls waiting because I was the fourth call five minutes ago."

The operator switched him to hold again. He stayed on hold for another two minutes and then he heard a sharp buzz. Disconnect.

He slammed down the phone. Why hadn't Krasnov called him? It was close to noon.

At two in the afternoon he finally got through to Krasnov.

"What did we buy it for, Krasnov?" he fairly screamed.

"Buy what? Who *is* this?"

"This is Aaronson. What did we buy IBM for?"

"Oh, Aaronson, IBM—20 shares. Just a minute."

And then a groan. "Oh my god—I forgot to put it in."

There was a silence at both ends, and then Krasnov spoke. "I'm sorry, Aaronson. It was chaos here today. I had every customer I've ever sold on the phone. I slipped up, Aaronson. Your buy order must have fallen to the floor. I'm terrible sorry, Aaronson, what can I tell you?"

"You can tell me what IBM closed at."

"122. It was up 17 points."

On the F train to Brooklyn, Aaronson got a seat across from a fat lady wearing a flower-print dress with her stockings rolled down below her knees. She smiled faintly at Aaronson. He opened the *Post* and read *Peanuts, Dear Abby,* and of course the stock market report. The biggest day in fifteen years.

At Kings Highway he got off the train and bought a Snickers bar and a Peanut Chews from the candy stand at the station. He gave the guy a dollar and got four cents change. Forty-eight cents for a candy bar—outrageous.

He went up to his apartment, had a chopped-liver sandwich and a Diet Coke for dinner, and then sat in front of his calculator, thinking. His fingers raced over the keys, the machine clicked and whirred, and it gave Aaronson a sense of extraordinary power. Maybe it was more power than a man was supposed to have, he thought. Maybe it was evil. Perhaps in some strange Faustian way he had sold his soul for the formula, as indeed many men would have done. Surely it wasn't natural. Surely it was some black magic that governed his calculator.

Perhaps Krasnov's error had been a warning. Perhaps it whispered, "Leave it alone, Aaronson." And Melchior, away for a week suddenly. Maybe someone was saying, "Don't touch it, Aaronson, it is not meant to be. It is not meant for any man to devise a formula to yield limitless wealth."

He thought then of King Midas, whose gift was not singularly different from Aaronson's but who suffered a dreadful punishment. And he thought about the punishment, and how the food turned to gold before the King could swallow it.

He thought about all this, and went to collect the three formulas: from behind the wallpaper, from the coffee tin, and from the book. He crumpled each one in an ashtray, lit it with a match and watched it burn.

Then he opened the refrigerator, got a hard-boiled egg, and went to watch *The Late Show.*

KRINSKY AND THE RAGMAN

Only one thing frightened Krinsky. Not the union, with their impossible demands, nor the bankers, arrogant and condescending. Not even the buyers who squeezed him for every penny. Only one thing frightened Krinsky: the ragman.

Krinsky owned a small shop manufacturing ladies' underwear. Every day the cutter spread a few thousand yards of cotton broadcloth on the cutting table, piling it layer on top of layer until he had stacked two or three hundred layers of fabric. Then the patterns were arranged on the top layer of fabric and the huge electric cutting knife would trace around the patterns, cutting out blocks to be used as sleeves or backs or bodices. In between these blocks were small waste pieces and these were piled into corrugated containers, awaiting the ragman.

Every week the ragman came to Krinsky's shop and collected the rags in burlap bags about the size of an oak barrel. The rags had value; they would be sold for paper pulp, eventually recycling themselves on to the front page of *The New York Times*. I remember that I always had the notion that the very rags that were lying carelessly in the cartons would soon appear before my eyes as a James Reston column.

We always separated the rags by fabric and color because certain fabrics were more valuable. Cotton was the best, but cotton blended with polyester or any synthetic brought down the price. Apparently pure cotton mashed into pulp most easily. And white was the best color. We used to get nine cents a pound for white cotton, but colors would cut the price in half. The ragman said that colored cotton had to go through a special process to bleach out the color. Otherwise, he said, *The Times* would appear on the newsstand colored pink or blue. I thought it made a lot of sense.

Sometimes the ragman would only offer us two or three cents a pound for colors and that always started an argument. Krinsky and the ragman would flail their arms, hold their hearts, wipe the sweat from their brows, and implore the heavens. The arguments never lasted long and the ragman always won. He owned the final word.

"Listen Krinsky, if you don't want to sell the blue cotton for three cents a pound forget about it. I don't make a cent on it anyway; nobody wants colors. I take it off your hands as a courtesy. If you want, I'll leave it here."

We couldn't let him leave it because we'd have to throw it out anyway, so Krinsky finally conceded. There was another reason why Krinsky conceded: He was scared. Actually we were all scared of the ragman. He was a gorilla of a man, not much more than five feet tall with swaying arms and huge tufts of black curly hair growing from his shoulders. He always wore an undershirt, smeared with the dirt of freight elevators and filthy burlap, and he always carried a meat-hook. His helper would hold open the burlap bag and he would stuff it with the contents of the cartons. Then he would knot the top and swing his meat-hook into the side of the burlap, digging it so deep into the rags that you could only see the handle. With the steel imbedded and caught in the belly of the burlap, the ragman could lift the bag with the meat-hook handle and toss the thing on a dolly.

Franco, his name was, and I was scared stiff of him. So were the rest of us.

On Friday, before the ragman came, Krinsky would always warn us.

"Watch what the ragman dumps into those bags. Everybody keep your eyes on him."

I did keep my eyes on the ragman but I tried to be casual about it. Once Franco said to me, "What are you watching me so closely for? You afraid I stole a box of underwear? Here, dig your hand into the burlap bag—see if you feel anything there that doesn't feel like rags."

I looked at Franco with the meat-hook slung around his neck. "No, no," I said, "I'm not watching you, Franco. I was just looking to see how you tie those ends of the burlap together."

"Well reach in there anyway," Franco said. "I want you to know that I don't screw around."

I didn't want to. It was humiliating. I knew there was nothing but rags in the burlap or Franco wouldn't be asking me. I would dig my arm down to the middle and come out covered with rag shavings. And then I'd have to admit there was nothing in the bag. Franco was making a fool out of me.

"It's O.K., Franco; I don't have to check on you."

Franco gave me his gold-tooth grin. "Dig your goddamn arm into the bag," he said. "I'm tired of all you guys watching me like I'm some kind of thief."

The brown dirt-sweat poured down Franco's neck, running over the slick metal of the hook. I reached down into the burlap. "Nothing there," I smiled, wet in the armpits.

Krinsky got a hold of me later and laced into me in front of everyone. "That's what you went to college for? To let the ragman make a fool of you? As long as you were going to reach into a bag, why didn't *you* pick the bag? Why did you reach into the bag that Franco wanted? You let Franco make a big showing about how honest he is when he probably has half our underwear stock stuffed into those other bags."

I turned away. Six months in the garment business— nobody ever said it was going to be easy—but humiliated by the ragman *and* Krinsky within the space of a half hour?

It was a serious and sinister thing the way we watched the ragman. After all, what could he steal? A box or two of underwear? The guys who ran the freight elevators stole that much every day. The truckers were known to open the sealed cartons, grab a few boxes, and seal them up again.

It wasn't that. It wasn't just the stealing. The ragman was a stranger, an intruder from the outside world invading our sanctuary. I suppose it traced back to generations of Jewish businessmen, cloistered in their private, segregated world of commerce, being invaded by the government inspectors or even the secret police.

It had to be, because there was nothing really scary about Franco. He was just another laborer, sweating out a living in the garment center. Why couldn't we trust him? And why were we intimidated? It wasn't Franco. It was us.

Krinsky always made a show of courage. "Keep your eyes on that goddamn ragman and watch out for his tricks. Don't expect him to reach into the *shelves* for a box of garments. What he'll do is slide a box into the rag cartons. Then, when he empties the rags into the burlap, the box pours in along with the rags. Even if you catch him he'll claim that the box was mixed in with the rags and it's not his fault. He'll say that his job is to empty the rag cartons, not to worry about what's in them."

Krinsky had it figured out pretty well because I guess he was a whole lot smarter than the ragman. What he wasn't was a whole lot braver. I could hardly blame him. Krinsky himself was just on the high side of five feet with the build of an accountant. He wore spectacles—not glasses, spectacles—with narrow gold rims that didn't fit so well. They were always sliding down his nose and he was always looking at you over the spectacles. Krinsky wore a white shirt and tie and a grey vest that was never buttoned. If Franco wanted to, he could have lifted Krinsky with one hand and stuffed him into the burlap.

But Krinsky was the boss and the boss must show courage, so every Friday, before the ragman came, Krinsky gave out the battle orders. It was us against the ragman.

Once Krinsky even went so far as to kick the side of one of Franco's burlap bags. I don't know why he did it; it was like kicking an automobile tire. You just do it to look knowledgeable. I think Krinsky did it to show us that he wasn't afraid of Franco. That he was the boss.

Franco narrowed his eyes and didn't take them off Krinsky. Krinsky went about his business, nonchalant, slightly puffed up with his own importance, as though that's what you do with a ragman; you kick the side of his burlap.

Krinsky got the most of his show of bravado. After Franco left with his six or seven bags of remnants, Krinsky let us have it for not watching Franco close enough. He knew it wasn't true, but it gave him a chance to call everyone's attention to his own surveillance. I was impressed. I wouldn't have kicked the side of Franco's burlap for no money. I could picture the meat-hook going through my leg, the point coming out the other side.

I thought about the ragman a lot that week, finally concluding that he must have been a little afraid of Krinsky. You can never tell about those things. Franco was uneducated, slovenly. He was a garbageman of sorts. Maybe he looked at Krinsky with awe and respect. I hoped so. It made me feel as though we had a leader. Here was this Goliath, ready to rip us all to shreds, but we had our David. And although our David was fairly puny, he had something in reserve—some mastery over the enemy. And after all, what did David have three thousand years ago? A slingshot—only a homemade slingshot—but it stood up against a giant.

I was almost looking forward to Friday. At nine-thirty Krinsky lined us up for battle instructions. At ten-thirty I opened the freight door for Franco who walked past me as though I was invisible. "Hi, kid," he said.

The corrugated cartons holding the remnants were always stacked in the same place under the cutting table and Franco walked over and pulled out the first carton, sliding it along the floor to the freight door, and then picking up the whole carton and pouring it into the burlap bag, held open by his pimply-faced helper.

He emptied three cartons that way with seven pairs of eyes glued right to him: the cutter, the spreader, the foreman, two shipping clerks, Krinsky and me.

I was closest to Franco, and when he poured out the contents of the next carton—there was no question about it—two blue boxes of underwear went tumbling into the burlap. You had to be close to see it because the boxes and the rags all poured in together. It would be like seeing fish in a waterfall.

Nobody said anything; I guess I was the only one who saw it. I was petrified. What do I do now? My mind raced like a motor and my face flushed. I debated walking up to Franco and asking him to empty the bag, or telling Krinsky, or doing nothing. Just then Franco whacked the meat-hook into the side of the burlap. I did nothing. But Krinsky was walking right up to Franco. He had seen it. He was going to tell Franco to empty the burlap. Holy mackerel—there was going to be bloodshed.

Krinsky strode right up to Franco. Daring. Too daring, even. But when he reached the ragman he gave the bag a kick and smiled. He hadn't seen it. It was just Krinsky doing his bravado act.

Franco didn't like it a bit but I was sure he wouldn't say anything. He had two boxes hidden in the burlap. He swung the bag on the dolly and then turned to face Krinsky.

"Hey, Krinsky, what are you kicking the bag for? You think I got something stuffed inside? You think I'm stealing your garments? You think I need to steal a few boxes of your cheap underwear? O.K. Krinsky, let's find out. Reach inside the burlap and see for yourself."

Only it wasn't the same bag that the two blue boxes were in. That bag was lying on the dolly. I hadn't taken my eyes off it.

Everyone was watching Krinsky and Franco and holding his breath. I guess no one was holding it tighter than me because only I knew how tense the situation was.

Krinsky looked Franco right in the eye, but it was obvious that he couldn't dig into the burlap bag that Franco pointed to. He had just finished tearing my head off last week for making that mistake.

"If you want me to reach into the bag, Franco, *I'll* pick the bag," and he motioned to the bag on the dolly.

Franco blanched and hesitated—then dug his hook into a different bag.

"Not that one, Franco, this one," Krinsky ordered, pointing to the danger bag with extrasensory vision.

There was nothing for Franco to do but pull the right bag off the dolly. I was hoping for a sign from heaven. A fire drill. An emergency call from the Sears buyer. Nothing came. Nothing happened. Franco made some feeble attempt at not being able to open the knot, but Krinsky held his ground and the knot was opened, the white cotton shavings spilling over the side.

"Phone call from the Kmart buyer!" I hollered. Anything to buy time.

I was still the closest of anybody to Franco, Krinsky, and the burlap bags, and I could see Krinsky turn white and hesitate when his fingers touched the cardboard box. I also could see Franco turn away, nervous and uncertain. About to be caught at the oldest theft game in the garment center.

And then Krinsky drew his arm out covered with white shavings. He looked at Franco and Franco looked at him, and they both stood there for a moment. And then Franco turned his head away a little, chagrined. And Krinsky turned his head away a little, and I could see how terribly frightened he was. "It's O.K., Franco," he said. "Close it up. There's nothing inside the burlap."

Franco tried to say something but nothing came out, so he stuck out his hand and Krinsky took it. I'll always remember that handshake: It looked like King Kong shaking hands with someone in the third grade.

The following Thursday, for the first time ever, Krinsky didn't line us up for battle orders, and on Friday, for the first time ever, nobody watched the ragman.

Three Square Inches
of Nothing

There were two factions in Clancy's Bar: the steelworkers and Vladimir. Vladimir was an art historian, a subject about which he would talk endlessly, in no way concerned with who was listening. It was fortunate, because no one ever was.

The steelworkers tolerated him, not because they enjoyed his company, but because they found him peculiar. It was something of a game to discover how peculiar Vladimir could get. He was a curiosity, a sideshow freak, who the steelworkers could neither live with nor entirely live without.

Clancy's Bar was home to Vladimir. He ordered a Tom Collins and expounded on the Renaissance. And finally, when one of the steelworkers told him to shut up, Vladimir told him to put up his dukes. This brought down the house because any twelve-year-old could have flattened Vladimir. The steelworker would accept the challenge and come over and blow on Vladimir. Vladimir would call him a Philistine, and the guys would scream, "Yeah!" and "All right!" Someone ordered a round of drinks, and the mock battle blew away like the head on a stein of beer.

In such a strange manner Vladimir became one of the guys. He had an identity, however bizarre, and he was at home. Which was why he drank at Clancy's and expounded on the Renaissance. It was his trademark and it was accepted. He would have been tossed out of any other bar in town.

One afternoon around five-thirty, Vladimir was sounding off. Nobody was listening, of course, but even then it was a hot afternoon and Vladimir was becoming bothersome. Carmine, who carried steel girders up the side of fifty-two-story apartment houses, told Vladimir to lay off. Vladimir said who's gonna make me. Carmine threw a crumpled napkin at him and Vladimir raised his fists. One of the steelworkers offered to hold Vladimir's coat, and six others pretended to hold back Carmine, who was screaming, "Let me at him!"

"And anyway," Carmine shouted, "you don't know anything about art. All your stories are a lot of crap."

It was one thing to call Vladimir a coward but quite another to impugn his knowledge of art history. He dropped his mock battle stance, stood up straight, and said to Carmine, "If you don't think I know what I'm talking about, why don't you bring in a picture of a painting—any picture out of any book—and I'll identify the artist. If I miss it, I buy drinks for the house. If I get it right, you pay for my next Tom Collins."

This seemed like a pretty good bet to Carmine, although at the moment he would have bet on anything. The deal was made, and the steelworkers went into a huddle about how they would choose a painting to stump Vladimir.

In fairness, the choosing was not an easy job. Collectively, they were familiar with a limited number of paintings. But it was clear that there had to be a few thousand paintings in the world, and certainly Vladimir couldn't know all of them. All they had to do was to find an art book, and since most of the workers had children in school, most of the homes had an art book on the shelves somewhere.

Carmine showed up the following day with a book on Italian painting, and the guys grouped around to make a selection.

"How about that one?" chimed McIntyre, pointing to the *Mona Lisa*, and anxious to establish his credentials in this intellectual wasteland. Fourteen faces turned to him at once. Asking Vladimir to identify the *Mona Lisa* would be an insult even to Vladimir, not to mention the certain loss of one round of drinks. So they flipped the pages for another few minutes, finally settling on something that looked very old and therefore very difficult.

Vladimir, only mildly to his credit, recognized it at once. He signalled for his Tom Collins, and the steelworkers regrouped to devise a new game plan.

The next day, Califano was ready with a tough one. He had asked his daughter to go through the book and choose something difficult, and his daughter thought that abstract art might be difficult simply because it seemed to her to have no specific identity. She pointed to a Mondrian, and that seemed quite all right with Califano.

It took Vladimir only a glance to recognize the Mondrian, his style being perhaps the most singular in modern art.

"Hey, what's the matter with you guys?" taunted Vladimir. "Didn't none of you ever go to school?"

The guys lowered their eyes and took it pretty well. It was fair game. A bet was a bet. You lose a bet, you take some abuse.

Randolph, the big black guy, promised to bring in the winning picture tomorrow. He was dating a school teacher, and any school teacher could pick out a painting that would stump the likes of Vladimir—or what was the school system coming to?

Randolph's school teacher chose the Impressionists, arguing to herself that although Vladimir would know the period he might still have trouble deciding between Monet, Sisley, and Pissarro. He did have some trouble, but not a great deal. Serve another Tom Collins.

The guys told Randolph what he could do with his school teacher and Randolph was rightly embarrassed. Meanwhile, the steelworkers were getting their ears pinned back and were sore as hell.

Vladimir was peculiar but not insensitive. He guessed that it was time to miss one and to buy a round. So he tightened the bet. He told the guys that they could show him a three-by-three-inch square of any picture of any painting, and he would guess it from that. Vladimir figured he couldn't win the bet, but there was always an outside chance, which is really all he wanted. He had already proved his expertise; now it was time to make sure he had a place to drink.

So the steelworkers went home, and Vladimir went home thinking about all the possibilities that might occur in a three-inch square.

The job of finding the painting was this time given to Kroloff, who represented that a friend of his wife owned an art gallery. Kroloff's instructions were to stump Vladimir on the three-inch square or to never show his face at Clancy's again. The guys meant it—almost.

That night Kroloff told his wife Agnes about the bet, and asked her to call her friend, which she immediately refused to do.

"You want me to humiliate myself in front of my friend by asking her to find a painting that will stump one of your drinking buddies? Worse, you want me to ask about a painting that you can show a three-inch square cut out? For godsakes I don't need an owner of an art gallery for that. Cut out a square from *any* painting. Who the hell do you have in the bar, Thomas Hoving?"

Agnes was right, Kroloff thought. And even if she wasn't right he was too embarrassed to pursue it.

"Well, all right," he said, "find me an art book and cut out a square and make sure there's no way anybody can figure out what it is."

Agnes was crafty but not terribly smart. She pulled down an art book from a high shelf and went leafing through the pages. As she considered painting after painting, searching for the perfect three-inch square, the job grew more complicated than she had originally thought. A three-inch square of a picture that is six-inch by six-inch represents one-quarter of the picture. In an area that size it seemed that some characteristic of the style showed through. There didn't seem to be anything that was positively non-identifiable.

She thought she had it when she came across Wyeth's *Christina's World*. So much of the painting was just grass field. But then, she reasoned intelligently, the painting was enormously popular, and if she cut out three inches of grass field, even a high school student might think of *Christina's World*.

So she flipped the pages, turning toward the back of the book, and she came upon Malevich's *White on White*. She had never seen it before, and it stunned her: an all-white painting, like a tile on her bathroom wall. She was not unfamiliar with abstract art, but she had never considered that an actual work of art, apparently well-known, could be nothing but white.

Her mind recovered from the shock and started to calculate. Indeed, a painting that had nothing on it! How could anyone guess a painting that was empty?

Alas, if she could only have traced her thinking back to *Christina's World*. She had reasoned that three inches of grass could only be *Christina's World*. Well then, what else could three inches of nothing be?

But she was too excited. The discovery had ignited her imagination. She could hear the guys saying, "Kroloff's wife found a painting that had three inches that were exactly the same as any other three inches." She could see Kroloff beaming, and she played the scene over and over.

She dashed in to show it to Kroloff who was amazed that such a painting existed. "There's no painting in that space," he said.

The guys at the bar were equally entranced, and the shock clouded all reason. It was not that the steelworkers were too slow-witted to recognize the problem. It was just that they couldn't grasp the concept of such a painting, thinking of it as nothing, rather than something. And it was also true that each one of them, in the back of his mind, was enjoying the discovery, and was fascinated with the idea of presenting to Vladimir three inches of nothing.

And so they showed it to Vladimir, and he *was* startled, but as soon as his mind started to scan twentieth century art, he came to it at once. Too quickly, in fact.

Vladimir considered three choices: He could identify it immediately—a humiliation. He could mis-identify it intentionally—a condescension. Or he could feign difficulty and then finally get it right. It fell to the third choice.

"What the hell is this?" Vladimir said. "Where is the painting?"

The guys beamed.

Vladimir flailed around, twisted and turned, cursed and mumbled. But after five minutes he started to focus. "Let me see…a painting that has three inches of solid white…nothing else. Maybe it has more than three inches of solid white. Maybe it's half solid white ... all solid white. I think there was a painting like that. I think it was called *White on White*. The painter? Malevich."

The guys were stunned, and their surprise turned to hurt. They lowered their eyes, turned away, and said nothing.

Vladimir bit his lip, cursed the goddamn guessing game, and walked out of the bar.

Now it happened in that time and in that place that there were two rather well-dressed gentlemen sitting at a table and watching the whole play unfold. And it happened, curiously, that they were associate professors—one of English, one of Fine Arts—at a nearby college. And it further happened that in spite of their education and intellect, they had no more brains than Kroloff's wife. And as a matter of fact those few brains that they had were about to get dislodged from their housing. Because they walked up to the bar, announced themselves as professors, and pointed out that Malevich's *White on White* was a hard painting to miss. And they pointed out, in addition, that they suspected Vladimir's delay in identifying it was nothing more than a put-on, maybe to sucker the guys into another bet.

And finally they offered to find a painting that the guys could present to Vladimir that would surely stump him, or the professors would pay for the round of drinks.

You can never judge the temper of the mob. On another day the steelworkers would have hung these wise-ass intellects from the overhead fan. But today they were down and a bit defensive. They agreed to let the professors choose, more out of indifference than commitment, and the professors immediately tossed around a few names which they were certain would stump Vladimir.

It was three weeks before Vladimir returned to Clancy's Bar, and when he returned he sat in a corner, saying nothing and blending in with the walls. It was another week before the professors and Vladimir showed up together.

The professors proposed the bet, but Vladimir just raised his hand signalling no more bets, nor was there any challenge arising from Carmine or McIntyre or Kroloff. But the professors, not quite sensing the anxieties, persisted. And somehow Vladimir didn't think he could refuse.

"You know, Vladimir, you can beat these guys with *White on White* but that doesn't put you much ahead of the twelfth grade. We were surprised, in fact, that you didn't disqualify yourself as soon as you saw the three-inch cut from Malevich's painting. That's what a gentleman would have done."

The professors went leafing through their book, muttering about Fra Angelico and Matisse, and finally they nodded and covered over the name of a painting that would surely defy anyone who would be drinking in Clancy's Bar. That *they* were drinking in Clancy's Bar did not occur to them.

It was a tough painting to identify, but not impossible. They might have found one that was impossible, but that seemed like more exertion than the situation demanded. They chose a Van der Weyden, *Descent from the Cross*, reasoning that the painting hung in the Prado in Madrid, and while Vladimir might have visited the Metropolitan in New York or the National Gallery in Washington, there was no chance that he had visited the Prado. They were wrong by three visits.

Of course, visiting the Prado and pulling a Van der Weyden out of one's memory are two different things. Vladimir struggled for a while, narrowed it down to the Flemish School, and finally guessed Rogier van der Weyden.

"That's absolutely impossible," said one of the professors.

"What's impossible?" asked Kroloff.

"It's impossible that he got it right. It's not even a typical Van der Weyden."

"Maybe he's smart," said Kroloff.

"He's not that smart. I wouldn't have gotten that right, and I *teach* Art History."

"Maybe he's smarter than you are," said Kroloff.

The two professors started to look around, at the ceiling, and into the bar mirror, searching for a hidden device. Meanwhile neither of them was ordering a round of drinks.

"One round—charge it to the professors!" shouted Carmine, and all the guys hollered "Yeah!" and "All right!"

"Just one minute," said one of the professors. It was an unbelievably wrong thing to say. A bet is a bet. A winner is a winner. A round of drinks is sacred. You might as well question God in the heavens.

Carmine lifted both professors by the collar, carried them out the door and deposited them by the curb, not far from the garbage cans.

He went back inside, walked up to Vladimir, and stood there jaw to jaw.

"Roger who?" said Carmine.

"Listen," said Vladimir, "one round for the guys; it's my turn."

Carmine held up one massive paw as though he were stopping traffic.

"One Tom Collins," he said to the bartender, not without a smile.

NOBODY BEATS MASON

I have to tell you about the extraordinary tennis match between Tony Mancuso and Mason Delacourt.

Mason is the number one player at our club, which is what happens when you learn to play tennis at the age of seven. At seven, in the country clubs of Greenwich, Connecticut, Mason had already developed a backhand. Most of the guys at the club, at the age of thirty-seven, have still not developed a backhand, which is one of the reasons why nobody beats Mason.

Mason is also beautiful on a tennis court. Like an eagle in flight, like a gazelle on the African Plains, Mason seems to the tennis court born. He's six-two or -three, lean, and incredibly graceful. He gets way down on his backhand and follows through on his forehand. His volley dies on the spot. His serve skips to the right or left. He is poetry and majesty blended, and just about everything all the rest of us would like to be.

It would be easy to dislike all that talent but nobody dislikes Mason. He plays with everybody, talks to everybody, and tells funny stories about how his father made him learn tennis when nobody had ever heard of tennis and all the guys were playing football and basketball. No wonder my serve skips, he seems to be saying. It makes us feel better, because none of us have a serve that skips, and we all secretly feel that if we had learned tennis at seven instead of twenty-seven we'd all play like Mason.

So Mason is our idol and Mason is our pride. When we bring a guest we point out Mason. When we talk about tennis we talk about Mason. When we sit around on the patio we sit near him and we listen to what he says. Mason always has stories about how Jack Kramer used to come to his club in Greenwich and play against the pro. And he always knows everything about the current players. "The fastest guy on the courts is McEnroe," he'll say. And someone else will say Becker. And Mason will say, "Well, maybe today. Maybe McEnroe's lost a step. But up to a year ago it was McEnroe."

And we would all nod at each other because that had to be the truth, and we would all feel safe about repeating Mason's stories to anyone.

Mason beats me about 6-2. I've never won a set from him. Once I had him 4-2 and I thought I might win it. It wasn't that I was playing well, because even if I played with divine inspiration I still haven't the strokes to beat Mason. But once in a while Mason will string together some errors and this was one of those rare times. He came out of it though and beat me 6-4.

After the morning games we sit around on the patio, drink Cokes, and talk about tennis. It's an important part of the day because that's when you can tell everyone that you lost to Mason 6-4. Losing to Mason 6-4 is better than beating anyone else. The object is to let everyone know about it without appearing pompous. Hopefully someone will ask you. If not, you have to force it. It's a cardinal rule that you never force it if you *won*. That would be incredibly bad taste. You just don't go around saying, "I beat Marty 6-1 this morning." But if you've lost it's possible to mention it. You might start off by saying something like, "I guess I'll never beat Mason." Someone might respond, "How did it go?" And you answer, "Well, I got four games." And everyone turns his head because that's the tennis event of the weekend.

Of course you have to be careful how you answer when someone says, "How did it go?" You couldn't just casually say, "Six-four, Mason." That would seem like you consider it a possibility that you can get four games from him. Bragging. Absolutely. Very bad. If anyone gets four games from Mason he had better show surprise.

A lot of thought goes into the after-tennis conversation. For instance, let's say you got badly beaten by a player who shouldn't beat you at all. You don't go around asking everyone else how they did. The result of asking is that you get asked.

Also, if you've just been beaten you don't drink your Coke in the busiest circle on the patio. Someone is sure to ask you. Better to walk over and watch one of the matches or maybe check out the seeding on the tournament chart.

On the other hand, if you beat someone who you have no business beating, you naturally squeeze into a crowded spot and stir up an absolute whirlwind of tennis talk.

That's the way it is. I can't help it. Am I responsible for the egos of thirty million tennis players?

Before I tell you about the extraordinary match, I have to tell you about Tony Mancuso. Tony's about five-six, very dark, and very Italian. He has thick tufts of hair on his arms and a handlebar mustache. He usually sits alone and he always seems morose and brooding. We call him— though not to his face because Tony is a very strong guy— the organ grinder.

The organ grinder learned tennis maybe five years ago when he was about thirty. He has terrible strokes, or at least they seem terrible, mainly because they are clumsy. Nevertheless, Tony beats most of the guys who have good strokes, and he does this because he is very fast, very determined, very athletic, and somehow manages to get the ball over the net all the time, which, like it or not, is what wins a tennis point.

Nobody sits with Tony on the patio and I think it's because Tony never talks about interesting things like whether McEnroe is faster than Becker. I know I don't like to sit with him because, among other things, he might ask me to play a set, and I *definitely* don't want to play a set against the organ grinder because he'll probably beat me on pure determination, and I'll probably have to admit it on the patio.

Mason doesn't think about things like that. Mason plays everybody. If you ask him for a game and if he doesn't have one, he plays you. I don't think he worries a lot about who is good and who is bad. Maybe, if I had a backhand, I wouldn't think about those things, either.

One morning I finish a match at about ten o'clock, and on one of the far courts Mason is playing Tony Mancuso. Nice of Mason, I think. I watch the match for about a minute and although I'm pretty far away I see Mason put a volley into the net, and I see Mancuso walk to the net to shake his hand. Mancuso shake his hand? Impossible. It can only mean one thing: The match is over and Mancuso won. I think about it a while. Probably Mason won. But no, there's no question about it. Whoever wins the last point *must* win the match.

They both walk over to the patio and sit down, but it's only ten o'clock and everyone is still on the courts. Mason wanders off somewhere and Mancuso picks out a seat in the center of a group of seven or eight chairs. I get a Coke and look for someone to sit next to, but the patio is empty except for Mancuso so I have no choice.

"Who did you play this morning?" he asks.

"I played Peter. He beat me in a tiebreaker." I might as well mention the score because he's going to ask me anyway.

Now protocol demands that I return the question. Certainly *knowing* that Tony just beat Mason it would be absolutely unforgivable not to return the question. Tony has just moved up the edge of his seat. He's almost smiling.

"Nice day for the beach," I say.

Tony slumps back in the chair but he doesn't give up. "Gee, you should beat Peter. How did it get to a tiebreaker?"

"Well, I had him 5-3. Missed eight backhands in a row. It got up to 6-6 and he won the tiebreaker."

"Did you ever play Mason?" Tony asks relentlessly. He has the conversation back on track.

"Yeah, I've played him. Sometimes I even get a game or two. Once I caught him when his back was all strapped with adhesive tape and I was ahead 3-1. I think he got a little irritated though and he took the next five games."

At this crucial point I get up and tell Tony I'm going to change my shirt which is pretty soaked. That's not why I'm getting up though—Tony is closing in. He's going to *tell* me about the match. I can feel it. He's got all the bait out and if I don't bite he'll tell me anyway. If I say, "Nice day for the beach," again, he'll say, "Nice day to beat Delacourt."

I can't stand the thought and I take off for the locker room. As I change my shirt I keep thinking, why won't I ask him? What's the matter with me? Why don't I say to Tony, "Who'd you play this morning?" Why don't I say it in front of seven of the guys? It would be around the whole club in fifteen minutes.

It would be a blessing. It would be heard in Rome and Jerusalem. And when I appear at the Gates, and when they ask me what I have done, my advocate could say, "He asked Tony Mancuso in front of seven guys." And O Lord, those gates would swing open because with thirty million tennis players this is no longer a game. This is a religion.

I begin to daydream and a picture flashes through my mind. It's Mason, playing tennis on his private court in Greenwich. God, how I would have liked to grow up in Greenwich. As it happened I grew up on the streets of Brooklyn—a stickball champion. Ten years devoted to stickball. If stickball becomes the new national game instead of tennis, I'll become Mason and Mason will become me.

My mind drifts from stickball to baseball, and to the bleachers of Ebbets Field. I'm sitting there between two mustache-types and feeling very uncomfortable. Suddenly Mancuso appears and hollers out a big hello. I make out like I don't see him.

I wake up and observe that my daydreams don't take much to figure out. Even my daydreams have no class. Some guys have poetic, sophisticated daydreams; you could write a book about them. My daydreams wouldn't even make the pulps.

But at least I know where I'm at, I figure. At least I know where I want to be. I want to be right here on the beaches of East Hampton, one of the loveliest places in the world. And I want to play tennis at this private club where a lot of the guys are lawyers and writers and advertising executives, and everyone is lean and sunburned and terrific-looking. I didn't just stumble into this—it took a lot of work—it took some brains, and even a measure of class. I'm here now; I'm part of this. Don't let this go, I tell myself.

It's afternoon, and I'm lying on the beach. Ron and Peter walk over. Am I going back to the club? Do I need a ride? Of course I'm going back to the club. Where else do I spend every waking hour that I'm not on the beach?

Ron picks me up in his Mercedes and we pick up Peter. Peter's trying out a new graphite racquet. We talk about graphite racquets. Mason uses graphite.

We reach the club and walk onto the patio. There are only two people sitting there; no one has returned from the beach yet. Larry is sitting in a far corner reading *The Times*. Tony is sitting a little closer. *Now* I'll ask him, I think. It's easy—I'll just ask him. But I can't. What the hell is this? A simple question about who won a tennis match and I can't ask him. Tony starts to rise as we enter. He obviously thinks he's the fourth in a doubles match. Somehow we gravitate toward Larry. Tony slumps back in his chair. Larry puts down the financial section and we all go out on court one. No one else is there so we naturally take the best court. Yet there is that awareness that we belong on court one.

Tony wanders over to watch. He looks so shaggy and forlorn. I'm aware of what I'm doing and I genuinely feel sorry for him. I guess I don't feel *very* sorry for him because it wouldn't take much to do something about it.

It's my serve. The first one goes into the net. Five hundred dollars in lessons from the best pro on Long Island and I still hit every first serve into the net. I get ready for my second serve and I catch Mancuso out of the corner of my eye. My mind flies back to Ebbets Field and I start to think of the hot dogs that we used to pass up the stands, hand-to-hand, overhead.

Ron hollers it's my second serve and what's the matter?

I don't know what's the matter.

I hit the second serve way past the baseline and stand there for a minute. I'm not sure what I'm feeling, but things seem to be getting a little clearer. Then I walk over and sit down next to Tony Mancuso.

He looks at me. "You O.K.?" he asks.

"A little tired," I say, and put a hand on his shoulder. "Why don't you take my place."

Tony smiles his organ-grinder smile and I start to feel better. Tomorrow I might ask him how he did against Mason.

DEATH BY PASTRAMI

Fleishman sold funerals. You don't think of funerals being *sold*, but of course they are, just like encyclopedias and municipal bonds. The funeral houses need business the same as the brokerage houses, and while business must inevitably come to them, the different houses compete for the same action—for the same body, if you will.

Funeral houses print business cards, advertise their services and hire salespeople. They also give discounts, similar to Macy's, although the funeral houses suffer no seasonal lulls. People die, after all, at a reasonably steady pace throughout the year.

This may offend a lot of people and I'm sorry about that. Dying is sacred and funerals aren't funny, but in fact business is business and the funeral houses have to make a payroll the same as everyone else. Which explains why Fleishman was a salesman at Excelsior Chapels, trying to drum up some action. Not hoping that people will die—you don't have to hope—but only wishing they will die in one of his caskets, preferably mahogany, on which his commission was considerably more generous than on the walnut variety.

Fleishman was not a high-powered salesman. High-powered salesmen work on Wall Street; funeral salesmen simply can't get a job anywhere else. Still, if they don't hustle and bring in the business, they might not even hold their jobs at Excelsior. So Fleishman was always on the lookout for ways to promote his services.

How can you promote funerals you might ask, but it's a silly question. If hustlers can promote land sales in the Gobi Desert you can certainly promote funerals. Indeed, it hardly takes much imagination to hang out in senior citizen homes, play a little pinochle, and hand out business cards. I mean, what are the people thinking about anyway?

Fleishman, however, was not even successful as a funeral salesman—a failure among failures. He looked like the month of January, and while people don't expect undertakers to resemble Tom Cruise, a snappy suit with maybe a polka dot necktie is not thought to be inappropriate. Such are the rules of dying. Don't blame me; I didn't invent them.

On a particularly sunny day in June—too pleasant for people to think about dying—business had ground to a halt and the boss was on top of Fleishman, asking what he was doing to stir up a little activity. If he had been doing something he would have been working for Merrill Lynch.

"Get off your rear end and get over to places where people are dying," said the boss.

"I should take a plane to Bosnia?"

"You'll be taking a plane to your retirement home in Miami if you don't start bringing in a few funerals."

So Fleishman started to think about where people were most likely to die, and where he might be first on the scene to suggest a nice burial, but no ideas presented themselves. Worried and frustrated, he happened to glance at a small newspaper headline which announced: PATRON AT CRITERION DELI PASSES OUT AFTER EATING A PASTRAMI SANDWICH.

"Ah ha," he thought.

Now it is true that anyone eating a pastrami sandwich in a New York delicatessen is taking his life in his own hands. The smoked pastrami, piled six inches high, defies any digestive system short of that of a Bengal tiger. The fat content is enough to shut off the arterial system for a month. Blood has as much chance of reaching the heart as a car has of getting through the Lincoln Tunnel on Thanksgiving Day.

So instead of camping out at the Blue Horizons Senior Citizens' Home Fleishman headed for the Criterion Deli, figuring that if people are not dying on the spot they can't have long to go. But of course not everyone was eating pastrami. Quite a few people were having cheese blintzes and others were having scrambled eggs and salami, and while these dishes are rarely mentioned in health manuals, they are not a certain indication of impending collapse. So Fleishman had to find out who was ordering pastrami, and this was accomplished by bribing the headwaiter who dropped off a small note at Fleishman's table that read "Table #6." Naturally, good taste dictated that Fleishman not approach the table before the sandwich was consumed, and in fact it had to be discreetly handled even afterwards, but Fleishman soon developed a technique for sliding his card in the customer's pocket without the customer knowing what it said— at least until he got home, if he got home. Anyone consuming an entire New York pastrami sandwich is almost comatose anyway and hardly in shape to read a business card.

One or two pastrami sandwich eaters passed out right at their tables and were rushed to Excelsior. Others collapsed a block away, and since Fleishman often trailed them for a while after they left the deli, these gourmets also ended up at the funeral parlor, much to the delight of Fleishman's boss, who was starting to look at Fleishman strangely, as though maybe he was slipping a little something into the pastrami. It demonstrated an astonishing naivete about the gastroenterological wallop of a pastrami sandwich, especially for a funeral director, who is expected to recognize those excesses likely to steer some business his way. Slipping something into pastrami might be like adding a few grains of arsenic to cyanide.

Fleishman was exquisitely successful for six months and would have probably become the first millionaire funeral salesman, until it was noticed around Excelsior that Fleishman had taken to buying his suits at Paul Stuart. The other salesmen followed him to Criterion Deli, posted a lookout, and bribed the headwaiter, since it is well known that headwaiters at all New York delicatessens take bribes, not to speak of the countermen, who you have to bribe just to get a sandwich cut. Fleishman's scheme became known and the other salesmen each staked out delis, choosing them according to the height of the pastrami sandwich.

Next, the other funeral chapels discovered the scheme, figured out why their business had suffered over the past half year, and sent their salesmen—also losers, all of them—to various food emporiums where the cholesterol counts could insure some activity. They started with the delis of course, but Excelsior's crew had gotten there first, so aside from those delis where the headwaiter was open to the highest bidder (quite a few, actually) the delis were soon used up. This led them to the German restaurants where a veal stew with red cabbage, while not entirely lethal, could surely be counted on to provide a customer sooner or later. A few French bistros, still serving cassoulet, got a little play, and certain appetizer stores on

Second Avenue, renowned for their chopped liver, noticed the arrival of a new clientele who appeared to have stepped directly out of a Charles Addams drawing. The action had turned so dramatically to gastronomy that the old-age homes couldn't find a way to get their dearly departed buried.

Remember, this did not increase the total funeral business which is limited to certain logistical realities, but it did change the way business was done. In every delicatessen and quite a number of restaurants there was now a guy sitting at a table eyeing the crowd. Diners soon began to look around, wondering whether everybody was eating or watching. It didn't make for gracious dining, and restaurants soon observed a marked increase in their take out orders. Even the headwaiters noticed that while bribes increased, their normal tips for acting civilized diminished as there were fewer and fewer customers to act civilized to. Top management became alarmed—even those who were doing a little spotting themselves—and insisted that the restaurants were closed to the funeral crowd. It soon got so bad that Fleishman couldn't find a place to get a bowl of noodle soup.

In time, the salesmen drifted away from delis and restaurants and started to hang out in places like Madison Square Garden, where, during an exciting Knicks game, a few citizens could be counted on to keel over. The crowd made it difficult to reach them though, and if the score was particularly close no one paid any attention. Anyway, the excitement generated by a basketball game is nothing compared to the arterial assault of a pastrami sandwich, and so the funeral salesmen gave up on the Garden and returned to the old-age homes.

Fleishman, considerably wealthier from his six-month head start, was nevertheless frustrated that he could not devise a new pastrami scheme. He noted that on Wall Street they invented new schemes every year—one year junk bonds, the next year derivatives—but it appeared that schemes in the funeral business were once-in-a-lifetime events. It depressed him and he finally gave up trying and returned to his old ways. But he found that he could no longer concentrate, could no longer play out a hand of pinochle at the old-age homes, and he forgot the punchlines of the jokes that he told to his customers. Weary and dispirited, he was like a great show of fireworks that has its moment in the night sky and then fades into ashes. People avoided him and he took to aimlessly wandering the streets of New York, without purpose and without direction. And one day he found himself shuffling downtown on 7th Avenue, passing the shops and passing inevitably the delicatessens. It was late... he was tired... and he was hungry.

Y-S-L

Ricardo swore that he would never again buy anything with initials on it, his own or the designer's. Why do I need my initials on things, he argued. I know what my initials are. His intensity somewhat upset his friends, who looked at him and thought, so don't engrave your initials, Ricardo; no one will care one way or the other.

Ricardo held his course religiously, and when they asked him, at the custom shirt department, whether they should embroider his initials on his cuff or on his pocket, Ricardo threw the shirt on the counter and told them he would henceforth buy his clothing in more enlightened shops.

Ricardo enjoyed shopping for suits because suits were easy. Nobody asked about initials. He was a stylish dresser with a flair for matching patterns, and on this particular Saturday, at Barney's Edwardian Room, he chose a snappy grey plaid with a deep red pinstripe. He left the suit with the fitter and brought the vest to the tie department.

"It demands a solid burgundy," the salesmen said. "Nothing else will do."

The salesmen reached under the counter, withdrew a satiny, wine-colored tie, and laid it with a flourish across the vest. He was right; it was perfect.

But as Ricardo's eye traveled to the point of the tie, he noticed three initials intertwined. "What's this?" he asked.

"Y-S-L," said the salesman. "Yves Saint Laurent. Our better ties are all designer initialed."

"That's very nice," said Ricardo, slowly turning the color of the tie, "but let me have one of your cheaper ties without the initials."

There was an edge to Ricardo's voice and the salesman proceeded carefully. "Ah yes, they do seem to have everything initialed these days, don't they? But I'm afraid that just at this moment we do not have a burgundy without initials." He knotted the tie, perhaps to bring Ricardo's attention away from the point, but of course he could not measure the fury of his customer. Ricardo was past thinking about the tie, and was deciding between returning the suit and strangling the salesman.

But the suit was just too smashing, and surely there was a burgundy tie around New York somewhere, so Ricardo turned away and set out to find one. The crusade took him on a tour of the city, and he did find some more-or-less burgundy-colored ties, but they were either too red or too plum. The precise burgundy—that subtle, elusive tone of a great Chambertin— was impossible to track down.

After a frustrating week, a marvelous idea struck Ricardo, and he raced back to Barney's tie department. He found the same salesman and told him he wanted the burgundy tie with the Y-S-L embroidered monogram—the same tie he had been shown last week. The salesman, remembering the incident clearly, brought the tie to the counter.

"Wrap it up," said Ricardo, "I'll take it."

"But..."

"Wrap up the tie, I said I'll take it."

The following afternoon, Ricardo appeared at the office of his friend Stanley, who manufactured embroideries. The S. & S. Embroidery Company, working mainly for the women's and children's lingerie and blouse trade, made a business out of embroidering various patterns and designs on material. The raw material was stretched out on huge frames, where thousands of needles would stitch tiny floral patterns into the fabric, almost as though there were a thousand women sitting in a row, each working on a single rose or a daisy.

S. & S. was a large company and Stanley was a busy executive, but of course he was not too busy to see his good friend Ricardo.

Ricardo laid his burgundy tie across Stanley's desk, pointed to the intertwined Y-S-L, and asked, "Is this embroidery, Stanley?"

Stanley fingered the initials, turned the tie upside down so he could examine the stitching on the underside, looked up at Ricardo and said, "I think so, Ricardo; why do you want to know?"

"Because I want to take the initials out, and if it *is* embroidery I thought you would know how to do it."

"Come on, Ricardo; this is me, Stanley. Why do you want to know? You going into the embroidery business? I don't care, Ricardo; there's plenty of room. We don't do stuff like initialed ties anyway. It's a specialty."

Ricardo looked at Stanley, and felt his face heat up. Why didn't Stanley understand, he thought. I came all the way across town to get these silly initials removed and Stanley thinks I'm kidding around. He was becoming increasingly agitated, but Stanley put his hand on his shoulder, and Ricardo quieted down.

"Listen, Stanley, I know it sounds peculiar, but I hate these goddamn initials on my tie, and I want you to take them out."

"Well first of all, that's not easy, and second of all I have a better idea. Why not buy the same tie without initials?"

"Now look, Stanley, I may be a bit peculiar, but I'm not stupid. If I could find the tie without initials, would I be wasting our time having this discussion? I can't find the tie without the initials, and I must have the tie."

"It's a scavenger hunt or something?" asked Stanley.

"I need the tie, Stanley; let's not go into it."

Stanley examined the tie, took a small needle from his drawer, and started to pick at the initials. Then he laid the tie flat on the desk and placed a small box about the size that might hold a wristwatch on top of the initialed area. "It's a magnifying glass," he said. "I have to see how closely the embroidery is stitched."

Stanley worked his various instruments for about five minutes, then stood up and handed the tie to Ricardo. "It can't be done," he said. "If I take the embroidery out it will leave large holes in the tie. And just in case you might be thinking that holes are preferable to initials, remember this: even the holes will spell out Y-S-L."

Ricardo snatched the tie out of Stanley's hand, turned for the door, and then thought better of it. "I'm sorry, Stanley," he said, "but this whole thing is so damn frustrating."

"It's just a tie," said Stanley, kindly.

That night Ricardo had a new idea. At Seventh Avenue and Thirty-Eighth Street there was a tiny sign in a second-story window that read: TIES HANDCRAFTED—BRING FABRIC. Ricardo passed the sign on his way to work. Surely a tiemaker would know the answer.

The old man wore a grey cardigan sweater and had a tape measure draped over his shoulder. He was a little ferret of a man, with thin, wispy, grey-brown hair, and quick, poking movements. He measured the tie with the tape, turned to Ricardo, and said, "You'll lose five inches and it will cost you five bucks—a buck an inch."

"What do you mean, five inches?" asked Ricardo.

The old man looked over his spectacles and blinked, as though he couldn't understand why Ricardo was asking the question.

"I mean, if you want to eliminate the initials, you must shorten the tie. What did you think I meant? I have to open up the tie, cut five inches away from the point; then stitch it together again."

"You don't have to cut away a whole five inches to get above the initials," Ricardo said.

"Look, mister," said the old man, wearily, "I've been cutting ties for thirty-five years. A good business it isn't, but that's what I do. If I was smart I would be doing something else, but I'm not smart. The only thing I'm smart about is ties. I may even be the smartest person in the world about ties. So when I say five inches, believe me. Don't forget, after we cut away the initials, we still have to hem the bottom of the tie. You want to ask about the five dollars? O.K., we could negotiate that a little, but the five inches is five inches."

"Five inches is a lot to cut away. The tie won't come near my belt. It will look like I'm wearing a kid's tie."

The old man shrugged.

Ricardo thought about it a minute, considered that he could knot the tie so that the narrow end knotted up higher, allowing the face side to come down lower. But finally it irritated him, and he gathered up the tie, thanked the old man, and went on his way.

He thought about many things, did Ricardo. He thought about how he might always wear a vest, and in that way no one could see the initials. The idea sustained him for a while, but finally he couldn't bear the idea of *wearing* initials. It didn't matter whether or not they were visible. He cursed the tie; he cursed Barney's; he cursed Y-S-L; and he cursed his friend Stanley. How can it be, he thought, that twenty years ago nobody embroidered their initials on things, and now everybody does? What in God's name do initials do for a tie? Is it handsomer? Is it classier? Is it more elegant? What is it?

But no answer came down to Ricardo, and he drifted off to sleep imagining a huge bonfire of initialed ties and shirts.

Alas, all things come to those who stand and wait. And one day soon thereafter, at Mannie Walker Men's Shop on Seventh Avenue, there appeared in the window the exact tie that Ricardo wanted. It seemed almost too good to be true, and Ricardo stared at the tie awhile. Was the burgundy precisely the right shade? Would he find initials somewhere on the underside of the tie? But in fact Ricardo knew the search was ended; it was the tie he wanted. The Holy Grail had been found.

So he went inside and asked a salesman how much it was, although he almost laughed at his question because the tie could have been fifty dollars and it would not have mattered.

"The tie is twenty-two-fifty," said the salesman.

"I'll take it," said Ricardo, fairly feverish with excitement.

"You have to look on the rack over there; you'll probably find another in the same color."

Ricardo turned to the rack immediately. There were many ties in the same fabric and style, but none in burgundy.

"We don't sell much burgundy," said the salesman with a yawn.

Little did the salesman know that at that very moment someone was plotting a very unfortunate accident, nor was it to be quick and painless either.

"Well, then," said Ricardo, "I don't mind taking the one in the window. I'm sure it's not damaged or anything."

"We can't take anything out of the window display…"

"Don't take anything out; just put a different color in the exact same place and sell me the display tie."

"We couldn't do that," said the salesman, his life insurance policy about to pay off.

"Why couldn't you do it?"

"Because André, our window designer, spends many hours planning the display and coordinating the colors. André is very temperamental—you know how window designers are—and he has a tantrum if his arrangement is disturbed."

(Also André, thought Ricardo.)

"Now listen; this is a bit silly. You have a tie in the window and I want to buy it. You're a men's shop—I'm a customer. Maybe I can speak to the owner."

By this time the owner had heard the increasingly heated dialogue and wandered over to Ricardo. "My dear sir," he said, "you must know that we would love to sell you that tie, and I would sell it to you in a moment, except that I would immediately lose André. André is a bother, but it is not worth it to lose him over a twenty-two-fifty tie. I would have no one to do the windows."

Ricardo eyed the owner, slowly, from top to bottom.

"I'll tell you what I can do," the owner said. "When the display is changed I'll put the tie away and you can stop by and pick it up."

It was not an unreasonable suggestion and Ricardo did not know how to respond to it. If he argued further, the owner might not hold the tie. So, fighting desperately to control his temper, he gave the owner his phone number and left the store.

"A most peculiar fellow," said the owner, a bit shaken up. "I hope I don't see him again." He crumpled the piece of paper and tossed it into the wastebasket.

And actually, he would *not* ever see Ricardo again, which was probably a good thing for Ricardo, and most certainly a good thing for the owner.

By the time Ricardo arrived home he was quite nervous and jumpy. He briefly debated going back to the owner and offering him forty-five dollars for the tie, suggesting that he give André half to pacify him. He also considered finding out who André was and explaining the situation to him. A temperamental guy like André would understand. Both ideas made some sense, but they both carried the risk of losing the tie. At least, right now, there was a good chance that the owner would call him as promised. If he made too much out of it, he might alienate everybody.

He thought and thought, and finally decided what he would do. If he had been less heated and more rational he would have delayed his plan, but no, the plan would be acted upon at once.

Seventh Avenue and Thirty-Eighth Street, at two o'clock in the morning, is not one of the city's crime centers, nor is it heavily patrolled by police. Here and there a drunk stumbles around. Once in a rare while a dress manufacturer, designing a new line late into the night, can be seen leaving his building. But generally, two a.m. is quiet on Seventh Avenue, as the street awaits the commotion and excitement of the following morning.

On this particular night, at just about two, there was the crashing of shattered glass. Someone heard it and called the Third Precinct, and the police were at the scene within twenty minutes. Someone had hurled a rock through a display window, the shattered glass sparkling like diamonds against a full moon.

The owner of the shop was called at once, and arrived at the shop by three-thirty. Before he got there, he knew who did it.

"I think I know who did it," he said to the first police officer. "We had a really crazy guy in here this afternoon. I even have his name, and I'm sure you have a record on him or something."

The owner dashed into the shop, opened the drawer where he kept his notations, but then it hit him. He turned to the wastepaper basket. Too late. The cleaning lady had already been in.

"Ricardo, Ricardo something," he thought. But there were nine thousand Ricardos in New York.

"Maybe you could tell us what they took," the officer said.

The owner looked around at the splintered glass in the window display, trying to recall exactly what was there in the afternoon. Actually, nothing seemed to be missing. He hesitated a moment and then said to the officer, "I don't think anything was taken but I'll know for sure in the morning."

"Probably some wino," said the cop.

And then the owner knew at once what was missing, and his eye turned to the burgundy tie. But there it was, exactly where André had draped it.

Night turned to morning, and the police set up a small barrier around the display window, and all the cutters and patternmakers and sewing machine operators remarked about what the city was coming to as they passed by on their way to work. The police returned at ten in the morning, but the owner had to concede that nothing had been taken from the window or was otherwise disturbed.

"Can you give us a description of that crazy guy?" the officer asked. "Something specific—something he wore—a monogram, initials perhaps?"

The owner thought for a moment. "No, nothing specific… nothing really unusual… no initials."

It wasn't until three in the afternoon, when the owner was picking the glass out of the display window, that his eye caught the burgundy tie. There it shimmered in the afternoon sunlight with the intertwined Y-S-L near the point.

About the Author

Leonard S. Bernstein is an author of five books, including *Getting Published* and *"How's Business?" – "Don't Ask."* He is also an executive in the apparel industry. He was born in Brooklyn, NY and currently lives in Westbury, Long Island. He graduated from the University of Michigan.

.